THE DRAGON PRINCE'S SECRET

ELVA BIRCH

Copyright © 2022 by Elva Birch

All rights reserved.

No part of this book may be reproduced in any form or by any electronic or mechanical means, including information storage and retrieval systems, without written permission from the author, except for the use of brief quotations in a book review.

ROYAL DRAGONS OF ALASKA

This book is part of the Royal Dragons of Alaska series. All of my work stands alone (always a satisfying happy ever after and no cliffhangers!) but there is a story arc across books. This is the order the series may be most enjoyed:

> The Dragon Prince of Alaska (Book 1)
> The Dragon Prince's Librarian (Book 2)
> The Dragon Prince's Bride (Book 3)
> The Dragon Prince's Secret (Book 4)
> The Dragon Prince's Magic (Book 5)

Subscribe to Elva Birch's mailing list and join her in her Reader's Retreat at Facebook for sneak previews and sales!

PROLOGUE

*K*enth thought he was hearing fireworks when he first woke.

It was New Year's Eve.

No, it was New Year's *Day*; he'd stayed up to watch the turnover with a rare glass of wine. His daughter, Dalaya, had dozed off just before the toast, despite all of her excitement about staying up late and her insistence that she wasn't at all sleepy.

Kenth was confused. It was dark out, and he could see the pale blue twinkles of Dalaya's nightlight through the crack under her door. He couldn't decide what time of day it was; at this point in winter, this far north, the sun wouldn't creep over the horizon at all, though it would brighten the sky near noon.

As he reached for his phone to check the time, Kenth abruptly realized that he wasn't hearing fireworks, and the light from Dalaya's room wasn't her nightlight at all.

Magic! his dragon hissed in sudden awareness.

"Who's there?" he called, surging up to his feet.

The sound that wasn't fireworks was a crackle like

flame and there was a searing light from beneath her door just as he heard Dalaya wake and give a thin shriek of fear.

"Daddy?!" she cried.

Kenth wrenched her door open in time to see a crackling portal appear in the center of her tiny room, opening like a split in the air to a sunlit room somewhere far away. He was blind in the sudden light. The figures that pressed through were dark and indistinct against the brilliant backdrop.

"There's the princess!"

"Look out!"

"Over there!"

One of the figures was holding a page of paper that he waved at Kenth as he said a word Kenth didn't understand.

Magic! his dragon warned again, too late. The paper burst into violet flame and Kenth was caught up in invisible bonds, suddenly unable to move or prevent the invasion of his house. He couldn't seem to speak, but he could snarl, and if he tried with all his might, he could move in tiny, incremental bits, like he was trying to move through resin.

He watched helplessly as a big man with short-cropped hair and an unidentifiable military uniform plucked Dalaya from her bed. She screamed and kicked, slipping from his grasp briefly to dash towards Kenth, who was all but frozen in place, raging inside. They caught her easily and carried her back through the portal, crying piteously.

"*Alto!*" a voice from the other side called, and the portal sizzled closed, cutting off his daughter's voice, ending the spell that was holding Kenth frozen, and plunging him into darkness.

"Dalaya!" he cried, flinging himself at the space the portal had been.

There was nothing left to show that it had ever been there, except for Dalaya's empty bed.

"Dalaya!" he cried again, circling the room for clues. The teddy bear that Fask had sent her for Christmas was lying, burnt, where the portal had formed. The rest of her toys, crayons, and clothes were scattered around the room, nothing looked out of place in the chaos of a five-year-old's room. It had been a surgical strike, using a terrific amount of magic according to everything that Kenth knew about the art, and they'd known exactly where to go. They had been ready to handle even *him*.

And they had called Dalaya a princess, which was something that only one other person knew.

Kenth dressed with savage swiftness and found his phone. It was out of power, but that didn't matter. Fask wouldn't take his call anyway, and this was business best done in person. He tucked it into his coat pocket and went outside, where he spread both arms and leaped up into the sky as a dragon, winging angrily south and east for Fairbanks.

CHAPTER 1

Mackenzie felt alone in the sea of strangers at the lavish late breakfast table.

They were all quite kind, offering her decadent seconds of amazing food and kindly overlooking the times that she fumbled some attempt at manners that she only knew from books.

But if the severe woman in a guard's uniform sitting at the end of the table looked particularly suspicious, it was understandable. Mackenzie had, up until just the day before, been working for the Cause, a cult run by a woman named Amara who had tried to steal the Alaskan's magical artifacts, kidnapped Prince Tray and Princess Leinani, and used magic to temporarily strip them of their dragons.

Mackenzie had helped the two escape, but no one really trusted a turncoat, did they?

She tugged her shirtsleeve down at her wrist, even though there was no real chance of the tattoo on her forearm showing. The axe in a simplified labyrinth was the symbol of the Cause, an indelible mark of her upbringing.

Even the wound in her side that she'd gotten during the escape couldn't erase the stain on her skin or in her soul.

When Tray and Leinani snuck out of the meal, followed shortly after by Leinani's nearly hysterical mother and consoling father, Mackenzie felt more bereft than ever. She didn't know anyone else in the room and she didn't know how to broach the topic closest to her heart.

Her purpose in freeing the dragon royalty had been to secure allies who could help her free Amara's other captives, but since the rescue late the night before, she had been unable to present her case. The kind older woman whose care she had been entrusted to had brushed off her tentative attempts at asking for access to an authority and instead had insisted that Mackenzie rest and have her wounds treated. Mackenzie didn't know how to explain the urgency of her real mission here without being rude. She tried to be patient and navigate all the customs and culture that she didn't understand.

Should she make an official appeal to Prince Fask, as the eldest brother? Or did that entreaty go to Prince Toren, the youngest of the brothers, but the first with a formal mate according to the Compact that governed them?

She had expected to be brought for questioning that morning, not served a decadent feast. She couldn't figure out the chain of command from their friendly joking. Though she was introduced to each of them in turn, even that seemed to be in order of convenience rather than influence.

She cataloged them in her head. Toren's mate was Carina, an American. Tania, also American, was the staid woman beside her with a cane over the arm of her chair, and her quiet, bookish prince was Rian, one of the middle twin brothers. Prince Raval largely ignored the conversation but gave a distant nod of acknowledgment when

Mackenzie was introduced around like an honored guest. Another man, Drayger, who looked nothing like the brothers, winked at her alarmingly when he was presented, and clarified that he was a bastard of the Majorca royal dragons.

The conversation ebbed and flowed around her, and while they generously included her in the small talk, observations about the weather, and general gossip about royals that Mackenzie knew vaguely by name, she had little to contribute.

Her side hurt, and she was plagued by her purpose.

Finally, as the breakfast vanished and the dishes were cleared away, the discussion came back around to more serious topics.

Fask eyed them all, and Mackenzie thought he looked as suspicious of Drayger as he did of herself. "I want you all to keep to the castle for a time," he said frankly. "With the new year, there has been a great deal of political unrest and we're doing damage control. There have been riots and independent media has been spinning us in a very...unfavorable light."

"Here in Fairbanks?" Raval said in astonishment. "The worst we get are people protesting the potholes like we're personally responsible for frost heaves."

"The Cause has been busy," Fask said. Then his gaze did fall on Mackenzie. "They've stepped up their rhetoric and there are private reports of several assassination attempts over the new year. We weren't worried about the protests in the past, but these seem to be more organized, more driven, more heavily armed. People are getting hurt."

Mackenzie felt her heart race and the rich meal was heavy in her stomach. Here came the interrogation she'd been expecting.

Fask's voice wasn't exactly unkind, but it wasn't terribly warm, either. "What can you tell us about the Cause, Mackenzie?"

Mackenzie drew a breath, prepared for this question. "The Cause has been around, more quietly, for many years. Amara was a charismatic leader, and she gathered a cult of followers who thought there was something more to the Small Kingdoms than just royalty and tradition. She was convinced there was a great conspiracy of magic and corruption. For a long time, she preached a path of rejecting magic and the supernatural as impure and evil.

"But her story took a sudden turn as she realized what magic could do for her, and she has changed her creed from the certainty that magic should be purged to the idea that she should control all of it herself. Our—their—purpose shifted from destroying magic to stealing it."

"You can't make a change that drastic to an entire religion, can you?" Toren sounded pretty uncertain for a prince.

Mackenzie hesitated. She knew what she'd witnessed, but she knew that it probably seemed like a weird fantasy to people who hadn't been on the inside of something as consuming as a cult.

Doubt sizzled in her. Would they think that she was *lying*?

"You can if you control all of the media for a select group of people." Rian was a more thoughtful-looking mirror image of his twin brother. "Tray said you worked directly for Amara."

"Yes," Mackenzie said without pride. "I was...her Hand."

"What did you do for her?"

Their curiosity was as logical as their suspicions. "I read magic. If I can see the spell, I can tell what it does."

"You mean, you're good at guessing what it does from what is written." Rian had a kind of pushy curiosity that Mackenzie associated with librarians. She trusted him instinctively because she trusted librarians.

"No," Mackenzie said quietly but firmly. "I don't guess. When I see a spell, I know what it will do. I know the words of power, the limitations, and deflections, even if they aren't written out explicitly. It is my gift." Amara had always called it a gift. Mackenzie had come to regard it as a curse, a terrible burden that made her useful to all the wrong people. Maybe, for once, she could be useful to the right people.

At her words, all of their heads swiveled towards one of the princes. Raval, Mackenzie remembered. One of the middle brothers, the one who was a caster himself.

"Is that possible?" Rian wanted to know.

Raval shrugged. "It's nothing I've ever heard of, but that doesn't mean it isn't *possible.*"

"Can we test this?" the woman next to him asked. Tania, Mackenzie remembered from the wave of introductions. She was Rian's mate, and she had an ornate cane leaning beside her chair. "Maybe show her one of your spells?"

Raval looked outraged, as if he had just been asked to undress in public.

"I am happy to submit to your tests," Mackenzie said fervently. They had to believe her. If they didn't trust her, they wouldn't help her. If they wouldn't help her...she didn't know what else she could do, and she wasn't willing to admit defeat.

"We could show her the Compact," Toren said lightly.

"She's not to be admitted to the vault," Fask snapped, and no wonder; Amara had tried twice now to steal the

Compact. "We will test your claim, but I'm sure that you are still weary from your ordeal and injury."

Mackenzie resisted touching the place at her side that still felt hot. It hurt less now, just a dull ache, but if she slouched in her chair, it sometimes surprised her with a jolt of pain.

She opened her mouth to thank him for the thoughtfulness and protest that she wanted to help and that there wasn't any time to waste, because—

The door to the dining hall burst open and a furious figure barged in, shedding snow. Tray and Leinani were right behind him, still dressed for the outdoors.

"Fask! Fask, you bastard, *where is she?*"

A quick glance around showed that everyone else was just as surprised as Mackenzie was, but none of them looked particularly afraid; this wasn't a stranger to all of the brothers, at least. There were guards outside the dining hall that sheepishly closed the door behind him.

The intruder was wild-looking, with long hair and a scruffy beard. He was dressed in a worn Native parka and his hands were in mittens. Mackenzie suspected by his posture that they were balled in fists, and Toren was rising to his feet. "Kenth?"

This was the brother she hadn't met, the second oldest. He looked like he'd just wandered straight in from months in the wilderness. He didn't pay any of them the slightest mind, striding directly to Fask and menacing over him. "Where is she?!"

Fask looked as shocked as any of them and he stood. "What are you talking about, Kenth?"

"No one else knew about her, Fask. She was stolen out of her bed this morning, through a portal, and no one else knew about her!"

Fask had a politician's voice. Mackenzie knew too well

those measured tones, that careful way of speaking. Amara spoke like that, and it set the hairs on the back of her neck to attention.

"Kenth," he said, "I have no idea what you're talking about. Calm down and tell us what's happening."

"Dalaya!" Kenth roared. "Someone kidnapped Dalaya!"

"Who is Dalaya?" Toren wanted to know.

"Dalaya is my daughter!"

That made a murmur of shock and speculation swirl around the table and Mackenzie watched in fascination as the people accepted this revelation with a range of reactions. Carina looked delighted. Toren looked dazed. Raval's brow was furrowed in confusion, and Tania and Rian were exchanging skeptical looks.

"You have a daughter?"

"Since when?"

"Congratulations?"

"What the hell?!"

A secret child? At least Mackenzie wasn't the only one who seemed to have no clue what was happening.

"Calm down, Kenth. Of course, we'll use all of our resources to find her," Fask promised, rising to his feet. "Captain Luke will get a team on it. A discreet team."

Kenth had not given Fask a breath of room as he stood and was still snarling into his face. "Who did you tell?"

Fask met his angry gaze with impressive serenity. "I know we've had our differences," he said firmly, "but I wouldn't harm a child, and I've kept your secret."

"Who would take her? Why would they want her?" Kenth looked like he might like to wring the answers from Fask's broken body, like he was on the brink of unleashing his fury on his brother, held back by his own bared teeth. Several of the brothers had gotten to their feet, and were ranged around the two like they were ready to haul them off of each other at any moment.

"Who kidnaps children?" Toren asked, horrified.

"Ransom?" That was Toren's wife, Carina. "People do dastardly things for money."

Amara. Amara kidnapped children. Children were easy to control, and their flexible young minds meant that they were susceptible to some of Amara's favorite tricks. Mackenzie stared at her plate, not sure how to volunteer the information, then lifted her chin. "Is she a caster?"

"What?" Raval, across the table, was the only one who had heard her.

"The child. Is she...is she a natural caster?"

All of the attention in the room was suddenly focused overwhelmingly upon Mackenzie.

"Amara...talked about getting a great prize at the new year." Had that only been last night? Time zones confused her sense of passing time.

She looked up to find that Kenth was staring down the table at her, confusion and amazement on his face.

"Who are you?" he asked in wonder. He seemed to have forgotten entirely about Fask.

"This is Mackenzie," Toren said. "She was recently rescued from a cult that kidnapped Tray and Princess Leinani of Mo'orea." He gestured to where Tray and Leinani were standing together in the doorway, still dressed in parkas and boots. "Mackenzie helped them escape."

"Leinani?" Kenth appeared to have been stupefied, and he was still gazing down the table at Mackenzie, who felt unnerved by his regard.

"Leinani was supposed to be Fask's bride," Carina explained. "She's Tray's mate, instead."

"You've missed a lot," Rian said wryly. "Most of it in the last few months."

CHAPTER 1

Kenth paid them no mind whatsoever as he pushed past Toren to stride down the table to Mackenzie, who sat frozen in her chair because she didn't know what else to do.

"Who *are* you?" he repeated.

Mackenzie looked up into his face, wondering if she had done something wrong. He was handsome, behind the scruffy beard and the stormy anger in his face, and his eyes were bright silver.

Before she could answer, he was hastily saying, "No, don't be afraid, don't ever be afraid of me. You're hurt!"

She was so tense that the wound in her side was burning again, fiery, and her breath was shallow in her lungs.

To her astonishment, Kenth dropped into the empty chair next to her like his knees had failed him.

"M-Mackenzie," she told him, though Toren had already introduced her, and she got the feeling that her name was not what he was looking for.

"Mackenzie," he repeated in wonder. "And you are *my* mate."

"I'm sorry, what?" Mackenzie was keenly aware that they were the focus of every pair of eyes in the room. Even the iron-faced guard, Captain Luke, looked like she was holding her breath.

"*Another* one?" Toren said quietly after a moment.

"Don't you feel it?" Kenth asked gently.

Mackenzie wondered if this was some kind of elaborate test, a method of initiation. "Feel...what?"

Silence answered her. Then Tania, Rian's mate, offered kindly, "It's a little confusing, I know. It's like you can feel everything he can, all of the emotions you have now, and those that you will have after you have fallen in love."

"It's the magic of the Compact," Rian said from beside

Tania, covering her hand with his own. "It helps the heir to the kingdom to find their mate and lets them know each other when they meet."

Mackenzie knew about the Compact, of course. It was, officially, a treaty that bound all of the Small Kingdoms in matters of trade and defense and succession. She'd always assumed that the *mate* that it referenced was nothing more than a fanciful title for the diplomatic marriage alliances that powerful countries made to ensure their security.

But she also knew that the true nature of the Compact was magic. Amara coveted control of the document with a passion that bordered on obsession, sure that it was the key to controlling all of the magic in the world, and she often spoke of the power she would have when she owned it.

Mackenzie looked around the table. Did they mean to imply that the mates were actually magic love connections, chosen by the enchanted document?

It certainly sounded poetic, and clearly they all believed in it, but Mackenzie felt nothing from this rather alarming and intense stranger facing her.

"I'm...I'm sorry," she said quietly. "It's part of my gift. Magic doesn't work on me."

CHAPTER 2

Kenth's mate was staring at him with suspicion and doubt, and Kenth couldn't blame her a bit, even though he was getting a head full of all their future feelings, and he could not deny his own overwhelming rush of emotion and desire or his dragon's laser-focused insistence that she was the one, their true future, their great love, and that everything was happening as it should.

Even with her gaze lacking any hint of recognition, she was unsettlingly beautiful, with wide, dark brown eyes in a lightly freckled face with high cheekbones and a strong, set jaw. Strawberry-blonde hair was pulled back from her face in a strictly utilitarian braid, flyaway strands of it in a bright halo around her head. She would be tall when she stood, Kenth thought, and slight of build.

A one-sided mate bond? She didn't perceive him this way in return, or share his own feelings? Kenth was deeply baffled. What did it mean? How would such a bond work? It was so confusing to know everything about her, and absolutely nothing.

Kenth shook his head and chose the more immediate problem. "Who is Amara? What cult kidnapped Tray and…Leinani?" He looked around to find that his brother and the strange woman had followed him into the dining hall before returning his gaze to Mackenzie. "Where the *hell* is my daughter?"

He felt her swell of guilt and pain, as well as all the valor that it took to raise her chin and explain. "Amara is the leader of a cult known as the Cause. She teaches that there is a conspiracy of magic and secrets, based in a corrupt system of governance, and she has followers and allies in many countries. There are several layers of the Cause, from the people who live in her compound and follow her, to a dark web of media influencers who spread misinformation and dissent. Amara never shared the real size of her operation with me."

If Kenth hadn't felt all of her misery and courage, he might have thought she was unfeeling about the facts she recited. Her voice was calm and her face was serene, but under the surface, she was a cauldron of emotion.

"Media influencers?" Toren scoffed.

Mackenzie gravely returned his gaze. "Media is a powerful vehicle for propaganda and the world is full of people who have little to lose, looking for faith and community wherever they can find it. Amara is very skilled at understanding and manipulating people who are genuinely seeking answers, and your secrets are not as well-kept as you might like to believe. When there is a vacuum of transparency, it is very simple to direct a population of people with half-truths and fantasies. Especially with a truth like this. Magic? Shifters? Dragon royalty in control of the most powerful nations in the world? Convincing poor and uneducated people that they are being subjugated by a rich and power-hungry elite magical class is part of her agenda. Taking that power for herself is the rest of it. She has magic, now, that makes her work even easier."

"Where do you fit into this?" Kenth had to ask.

Mackenzie was silent for a moment, obviously choosing her words carefully, and Kenth had to fight his instinct to reach for her. "I was Amara's Hand. I helped her understand the magic items that she found and stole...and more recently made."

"She has casters?" Raval demanded.

Kenth really did reach for her hand then, because Mackenzie's anger and outrage boiled up so hotly that he was alarmed for her. His touch made her flinch back, which hurt the wound in her side and Kenth took his own hand back too quickly.

That's not awkward, Kenth thought wryly, realizing how it had to look and aware of Fask watching them. He told himself firmly not to let himself touch her again without invitation, even while he—and his dragon—longed to take her entirely into his arms and comfort her. Comfort *himself?* It was confusing in his head and he had trouble sorting his own feelings from hers, and *now* from some future that lay before them.

"She doesn't have casters, she has *children,*" Mackenzie said fiercely.

"She has *children* writing spells for her?" Raval and Rian exchanged a puzzled look.

"How does that even work?" Rian wanted to know.

"It would explain the handwriting," the woman by Rian said thoughtfully. Tania, Rian's mate, was a librarian from the United States who had been studying the true version of the Compact. *Two* of his brothers had unexpectedly been tapped with mates.

There were three now, if he included himself. No, *four*, because Tray and the Mo'orean princess were apparently mates. What did it all mean?

Mackenzie was continuing, "Amara found an ancient artifact, a stone that focuses magical intention, enhancing any natural casting ability that a person might have, but it only works on a mind with a certain amount of youthful flexibility and natural talent. It allows her to put them in a deep trance where they can copy spells for her, not have to craft them from scratch. Instead of a week or a month of heavy concentration, a spell might be written out in only a day. But...I didn't like what it did to the children. It exhausted them. It wasn't right. They just sit at desks all day, copying spells like golems or robots."

"Dalaya can't write," Kenth said. "She's only five. She can do her name and letters, that's all."

He felt Mackenzie's honest surprise. "Oh, I assumed she was older. Is she a...dragon? It is possible Amara wanted her for...other reasons."

Kenth felt her hesitation and disgust and the tension in the room ratcheted up another notch. "I'm missing something else here!" he said, angry to be left out when it concerned his own daughter. Mackenzie's flare of fear at his tone made him gentle his voice. "What would Amara want with a dragon?"

It was Tray who answered, his voice absolutely flat. "Amara can strip a dragon from a person and drain their power."

Kenth shuddered at the idea, and his dragon recoiled in horror.

"Not drain their power, *exactly*," Mackenzie corrected, though Kenth could see that she was wound so tightly now that her hands were trembling. He didn't have to imagine how much courage it was taking her to speak. She was deeply afraid of all of them but absolutely determined to continue and she had a clear and focused purpose that was driving her forward. Kenth couldn't tell what it was—maybe the kids?—but he knew that she would risk anything for it.

She faced Fask. "It's more like caging them in order to open the door to magic, to keep a spell going much longer than it ought to be able to, to reach further, and do more. Spells have a limited amount of magic to tap. Dragons appear to be a link to a more direct and inexhaustible energy source. That's what Amara wants."

"Dalaya isn't a dragon," Kenth said, frowning. "Not yet, though she's at the age that it could happen."

"She's likely to be a dragon," Fask said. "Her father is, even if her mother—"

"Don't talk about her mother," Kenth warned him, and only Mackenzie's alarm kept his voice from rising further.

Fask growled back, "I wasn't going to—"

To Kenth's surprise, it was Toren, the youngest, who stepped forward. "Okay, guys, let's agree that surprise-daughter Dalaya is gone, we don't know that Amara is behind it, but it seems likely. Let's focus on what we can do to do to get her back."

"When did you turn into a peacekeeper?" Kenth asked him, casting him a surprised and faintly grateful glance.

"I thought I was going to have to be king," Toren said honestly. "Everyone is really glad there are a lot of other choices now. Including you, apparently."

In all the rest of what was happening, that had not occurred to Kenth.

He was the *oldest* of the brothers with mates now, and

that put him in line for the throne. He could not resist a glance at Fask. No wonder his oldest brother looked like he was chewing glass. As irritating as it must have been to be passed over by the Compact three times for their younger siblings, the last person in the world that Fask would want to bend his knee to was Kenth.

The satisfaction of the idea was not worth the weight of the crown.

There was also the wrinkle that the Compact had chosen the other brothers first, and that Mackenzie herself didn't recognize the bond. Kenth could not resist looking at her again, at the soft, tense lines of her jaw, at the halo of strawberry-blonde hair that was escaping her simple braid. She had high Slavic cheekbones and haunted dark eyes.

"How do we find Amara?" he asked her. "How do I get my daughter back, assuming that is who has her?"

Sympathy. There was no doubting Mackenzie's helpless sincerity when she said in despair, "I don't know. I didn't plan to leave them behind in the first place!"

Kenth could feel how her side was burning with pain and he balled his hands into fists so that he didn't accidentally reach for her again.

"I was only going to help Tray and Leinani get away so that they could send help; I thought I could contact them again from within. Amara never trusted me with the details of her alternate locations. A big part of her strategy is to keep everything compartmentalized."

"Can we trace them with the financial holdings?" Tray suggested unexpectedly. "Amara said that Carina was the one who caused her a lot of trouble when she uncovered the fraudulent accounts at Amco Bank. Can we use that information to find out what else she owned?"

Carina shook her head regretfully. "Even if Amco *hasn't*

scrubbed that kind of information out of their records as they tried to cover their tracks, we'd have no way of getting it out of them without a lengthy lawsuit. The case is still stalled in red tape. Who even knows when it will go to court."

Carina was Toren's wife now, Kenth remembered. He'd sent a gift of carved ivory and a handwritten apology for not attending their wedding, not willing to leave Dalaya or risk his cover in the small town where they lived by being seen at the event.

The usual routes would take too long to save his daughter, Kenth thought, bowing his head and trying not to let his fear and grief overwhelm him. He had failed Dalaya. He wished there were something he could dismantle in front of him.

"Oh!" Leinani suddenly exclaimed, and for a moment, Kenth thought she had a rodent in her mitten, she hastened to tear it off in such alarm.

"The ring?" Tray said, just as Leinani pulled an engraved silver circle from her finger. He wildly shoved plates and silverware out of the way and Leinani put the ring in the cleared space as they crowded close to it.

"What—?"

"Is that—?"

"Are you—?"

"Quiet!" Tray commanded, and Kenth had only a moment to think that Tray, as well as Toren, had undergone some pretty significant personal growth since they'd last seen each other. His voice was crisp and he was completely focused, not at all the lazy prankster that Kenth had left behind.

The room went quiet and everyone leaned in to hear rustling and faint, distant voices. Kenth could barely make out the words, even sitting close by.

"It's not English," he said in disappointment.

"Wait for it," Tray warned him.

"Can we attach it to a Bluetooth speaker?" Toren joked, but he quieted quickly as the voices resolved, somewhat louder, and now speaking English.

"We lost a few of the parts," a male voice complained. "What's left is in that box."

Another voice swore. "Dammit, I just finally got that system set up just right and now I'm going to have to start all over again from scratch. How much damage can two demons and that spooky girl actually do? We should have just stayed at the last place. I'm sick of moving. I'm sick of being the only person in this whole damn compound who can boot a computer. I should…" The voice became muffled as it sounded like the person speaking moved away and the conversation grew indistinct.

"The other ring was in a bowl full of computer components," Tray explained quietly.

"You'd better watch what you say," the first voice said after a moment, sounding appalled. "Amara knows best, and she said that their escape was part of their plan. There would be punishment for suggesting otherwise."

"I obey the Cause," the second said repentantly. "Do we have a midi connector?"

"She says that the new brat will restore her full power," the first reminded him coaxingly. "Maybe our time of triumph really is at hand. Check that box over there."

New brat? *Dalaya?* Fury swamped Kenth. That was his *daughter*.

Mackenzie's alarm was the only reason that Kenth recognized that he had snapped off the top rail of the chair he was holding. He dropped the broken wood with a clatter that got him a hiss of warning from the others because the voices were going on, if quieter now.

For a time, they only spoke of computer components, clearly composing an inventory of the hastily packed boxes. Tania had produced a notebook from her pocket and was taking notes, but it was obvious that most of the information was useless; if the two cultists had any notion where they were, or knew any helpful details of their new compound, it was not coming up in their casual conversation.

"What's this?" one of them asked, their voice suddenly loud and clear.

"Looks like a ring," the other said. "Something magic?"

"Must have been packed here by mistake," the first said. "Amara will want that."

"You want to take it to her?" the second asked cautiously.

"I'll let you have that honor," the other chuckled. "You can take it with the bill for the new equipment to soften the blow."

"Thanks," the second said sarcastically. The conversation went muffled and then silent, as Kenth guessed that the other ring was tucked into a pocket.

Kenth let his fist hit the table, startling everyone and making the ring and cutlery jump. "That was useless," he raged helplessly. "We didn't learn anything."

"The ring doesn't activate unless there is information of use," Leinani said mildly, collecting her ring and folding it into her hand. "So, the magic thought it was important."

"We're more sure that Amara has Dalaya," Tray pointed out. "That's something."

"But we don't know *where*," Kenth said, trying hard not to shout. He was aware of Fask, always calm and composed by comparison. "So how does that help?"

"They probably don't still have our ice bucket," Rian said cryptically.

Mackenzie seemed to flutter in his head, a curious little ripple of possibility. He turned to look at her, caught all over again by the beautiful planes of her face and the depth of her eyes. How could someone look like such a stranger and feel so familiar?

CHAPTER 3

Reading a spell had always come naturally to Mackenzie. She pretended to Amara that she had to translate the words in order to unravel a spell, because reading had given her so much freedom from the rigid propaganda of the Cause and she didn't want that to be taken from her.

But she didn't actually need to see the words at all.

When she was in the presence of magic items, she felt like she could step into a room in her own head, a room with a mirror that showed her a wobbly reflection of her own self. In this place, she could see what would happen, testing all the possible outcomes. Activation keys and words of power bubbled up in her mind like dumplings rising to the surface of a boiling soup, the structure of it obvious and elegant.

With a little concentration now, she could caress the ancient magic of Leinani's magic ring and see it, like a beautiful piece of clockwork in her head. It was a gorgeous spell, especially compared to the hasty and simple spells that Amara relied on so heavily. It was growing faded with use, as if the teeth of its gears were ground down, but it still had several uses left. And not all of the uses were the ones that Leinani already knew about.

Mackenzie screwed up her courage. This was her chance to prove herself, to demonstrate her gift and make herself useful. "May I see the ring?" She held her hand out to Leinani.

Leinani hesitated a moment, then handed the ring to Mackenzie, who lifted it to peer at the tiny writing engraved all over it, keeping her cover story of needing to inspect a spell's words out of habit more than anything else. She glanced at Kenth, who was still gazing at her in a terribly unsettling way, and wondered if he would pick up on that tiny dishonesty. She found herself bothered by the idea of keeping anything from him, then reminded herself that she didn't know him at all. It was only that she was weak for the idea of a handsome prince enspelled to adore her.

"It's a listening device," Leinani said, as if that part had not already been proved. "Paired to the other ring that I had."

"It's more than a listening device," Mackenzie said, more confidently now. "It can also act as a locator."

This earned her a murmur of surprise and doubt that rippled through the room.

Leinani looked at her skeptically. "My mother didn't tell me it did that."

"It's a complicated artifact," Mackenzie said. "And very old. From the time of the Compact, maybe. Do you have a map? It only has a few more uses in it."

"Does it have to be paper?" Toren wanted to know. "I've got a tablet."

"The spell is not specific," Mackenzie said, testing the parameters.

Toren placed the tablet on the table with a map program open and Mackenzie handed the ring back to Leinani. "Anyone can use it," she said shyly. "You'll feel a pull to the right location."

Leinani put the ring on the screen, then swept it side-to-side. "Oh!" she said after a moment, giving Mackenzie a surprised look. "I didn't know it would do that." She pushed it to a corner of the map, then enlarged it, gradually increasing the scale until she had encircled a sprawling building on a satellite image of a jagged island in the Atlantic ocean.

"Where is that?"

Toren was trying to read it upside down. "Faroe Islands? It's not Small Kingdoms, it's..." he scrunched his eyebrows together. "Danish territory, I think."

"Fancy you knowing that," Tray teased.

"You would not believe how I've been cramming," Toren said grimly. "Ask me about royal lineage! I know about six generations of all the Small Kingdoms."

Rian was searching for the location on his own tablet. "That's a hotel, by the looks of it. 'The Island View.' It's been closed for a few years."

"Darn, I was planning to vacation there," Toren said.

Even Mackenzie could tell that his joke failed to land.

"What kind of defenses does it have?" Kenth's voice startled Mackenzie. He was standing so close to her it was loud in her ears, even though she suspected that he was trying not to yell. He seemed so angry and distressed that she was automatically afraid; angry people meant punishment, in Mackenzie's experience, whether that anger was targeted at her or not. She had no reason to believe that things would be different here, despite the kindness they had shown so far.

She watched Kenth from the corner of her eye, cautiously.

Was she really his mate? He certainly seemed aware of her emotions, and he'd known that she was hurt. She could certainly imagine no reason that anyone would invent such a claim; she was more a burden than a prize.

He was glaring at the map now.

"It's a hotel, Kenth. There won't be turrets or moats," Rian scoffed. "It's just big building on the side of a mountain with a nice view."

"That doesn't mean no defenses," Tray said sourly. "Mackenzie?"

Mackenzie stuffed back her alarm as everyone looked at her again. Was Kenth subjected to her every little insecurity and terror? She spoke as calmly as she could manage. "Amara will likely have only her most trusted guards and a handful of loyal cultists with her, if she's had the rest of the Cause go into hiding. It's always been part of her operation to be able to disappear quickly. They are well-armed and will have magic to shield them and defend the structure."

"What are the spells?" Kenth asked. "Do you know what all of them are?"

Before Mackenzie could answer, Fask said, "Since we know where she is, let's reach out and try to make a bargain."

"A *bargain?*" Kenth growled in disbelief. "You want to *buy* my daughter back?"

"It was just pointed out that a lot of her assets were evaporated," Fask said sensibly. "We have money. That might be a great motivation. We can take punitive action when Dalaya is safely out of the way, if it's still necessary."

"You don't bargain with a madwoman," Kenth

snarled. "And you can't statesman your way out of everything!"

Tray made a matching growl. "She's not going to treat fairly," he agreed.

Leinani, close at his side, was shaking her head. "She's not interested in money," she said softly. "Only power. *Control.* She has an endgame."

"What do you suggest, then?" Fask snapped. "An all-out attack on foreign soil? Fly in as dragons and flame the building to the ground? All you would do is endanger Dalaya and cause an international embarrassment!"

"I don't give a damn about embarrassment!" Kenth yelled. "She has my daughter!"

Mackenzie had been watching for a place to speak, desperate to make her case, and she took the tiny moment of lull after Kenth's outburst with all of her courage. "The other children!" she blurted. "You can't leave the other children there to suffer. Amara won't let them go for money, she's not interested in anything but power and nothing you can offer will be more than a delay tactic."

Fask looked at her with active distrust now. "We don't *know* that there are any other children. All we have for this is your word. All we know about their defenses comes from you. It's convenient that you happened to release Tray and Leinani. Convenient that you knew how to operate the ring as a locator. Maybe it's all a trap. There are plenty of people who would benefit from an incident like this. Maybe you're the one leading us on wild misdirection."

Leinani made a small noise of diplomatic protest, but it was Kenth who stepped up to defend her.

"She's not!" he said ferociously. "Mackenzie is telling the truth, the absolute truth, and she's been nothing but brave and selfless and honest and if you say one more word against her, I will show you the color of your blood, brother or not."

Mackenzie bit her lip, stunned by Kenth's emotional defense more than Fask's accusation. She wasn't sure she'd actually believed that she was his mate. Knowing her feelings was one thing, but it hadn't been as persuasive as this. The conviction in his voice was undeniable.

He believed her. He trusted her.

Did she have a chance at this after all?

Tears gathered in her eyes and she willed them back with all her might, trying to focus on her purpose. "Please," she said, hearing how pitiful it sounded. "Please do something to get those kids out of there."

Fask was frowning and shaking his head. Mackenzie wasn't sure if it was disbelief or just denial. "We don't have enough to go on. I'm not going to authorize an assault without more information. We don't need to start a war with Denmark and there's no use going in blind. I'm not saying that we're not going to do anything," he said placatingly to Kenth, "but we're not going to do anything *rash*."

Mackenzie didn't need a mate bond to know that Kenth was on the brink of an explosion next to her and she was tempted for a moment to reach out to him and try to calm him down.

Before she could do more than wonder at her impulse to touch a prince, he was throwing the rest of the chair he'd broken down on the ground to break into pieces.

"You're a fool and a coward!" he roared. "I should have known you'd lie down and show your throat when there was a challenge."

"What do you want me to do?" Fask demanded.

"Anything but run away!" Kenth snarled.

"You should know all about running away!" Fask shouted back. "That's what you do best!"

"You should be glad that's the path I chose," Kenth retorted, the rest of his threat unspoken.

For a tense moment, Mackenzie was sure that they were genuinely going to come to blows. Kenth balled up his fists and took a threatening step forward.

"Guys—" Toren said cautiously. The other brothers were edging forward and Leinani gracefully took several steps backward out of their proximity.

Mackenzie realized she was going to be in the range of their inevitable fight and just as she looked around for her own escape route with a spike of fear, Kenth directed his sizzling gaze to her and she watched his entire face soften. He lowered his fists.

Fask gave a little sneer. "Good choice."

Kenth swept past him, using his entire body to check his brother violently into the table before he stormed out the door that he'd come in.

"I'm not coming to save your ass if you do something stupid!" Fask flung after him and the door slammed between them.

The entire room was silent in the wake of Kenth's noisy exit. Mackenzie sank back down into her chair, trembling and unsure that her legs would continue to support her.

It had taken all of her courage to speak out and she felt like whatever bravery had carried her this far had abandoned her entirely. It probably had nothing to do with Kenth's departure, besides the fact that he was her greatest surprise ally.

"You didn't have to be such a jerk," Toren said to Fask. "His daughter was just kidnapped."

Fask gave a noisy sigh and Mackenzie thought he looked regretful. "He brings out the worst in me," he said. It was *almost* an apology.

"Everyone has been under considerable stress," Leinani said serenely. "We can continue this conversation again when tempers have cooled." She tipped her head to the general company with perfect royal manners. "My thanks for the breakfast. Now, if you will please excuse us…"

She sailed out with Tray at her elbow, and Mackenzie marveled at her aplomb.

She wasn't the only one who thought so. "Can't *she* be queen?" Carina said into the tense atmosphere. "That was very queenly. Super queenly. Way more queenly than me."

There were chuckles all around as everyone gradually relaxed, and conversations resumed.

Drayger, who had been on the far side of the table during the near fight, added, "Ah, all this tension takes me right back to all our family dinners. Just need a few poisoned drinks and a little more back-stabbing and it would be a proper Majorcan extended family reunion."

CHAPTER 4

Kenth stormed to the front windows of the reception hall and put his fists upon it. He knew better than to try to shatter it. It was three panes and while he could have broken through ordinary glass easily with his dragon strength, this, like so much of the castle, was enspelled for strength and clarity, resistant to frost and attack.

He could really use some clarity about now, he thought furiously. His heart was hopelessly confused, between the aching loss of Dalaya, who was probably frightened and maybe hurt, captured by a madwoman, and his newfound Mackenzie, all the layered permutations of her already fused to his very soul.

Fask was a short-sighted fool. This was their chance to sweep in with swift justice and free Kenth's daughter and the other children who had been captured, but Fask mistrusted Mackenzie. He mistrusted everyone because he'd never been trustworthy himself. He was so afraid of looking bad, he always played it safe.

They had always been like water and oil, Kenth

resisting his older brother's imperious direction and acting more reckless than necessary just to needle him. It had been little more than sibling rivalry at first, but the death of their mother had charged their relationship to active antipathy. Fask *blamed* Kenth for not being there to save her. Kenth didn't actually blame himself any less, but it poisoned any warmth that had remained between them.

And then, Dana...

Kenth made himself unclench his fists and put aside his anger, leaving his fingers splayed across the glass. He had Dalaya to think about first.

He could go himself, now that they knew where Amara was. A surgical strike, a lone wolf...or in his case, a lone dragon. The Faroe Islands weren't protected land; the Compact couldn't stop him from flying to Amara's stronghold and dismantling it brick by brick if he had to. Then...?

Someone's coming, his dragon warned, just as Kenth heard the footsteps. It wouldn't be Fask. Fask never followed anyone; it made him look weak. Toren and his mate, maybe, come to play at his new role as a diplomat?

To his surprise, his shadows were Tray and Leinani, hand in hand, with matching grim expressions as they walked swiftly across the hall to him.

"We'll come with you," Tray said when they were close.

Kenth felt the armor on his heart creak. He *did* still have family here, and Tray's loyalty touched him. "I don't know what you're talking about, brother," he growled, giving him a chance to back out.

"You aren't going to leave your daughter and those children in Amara's hands," Leinani said serenely. "And Amara's people found my ring. It won't be long before she guesses that we know where she is."

"We can't wait for *diplomatic measures* and give her a chance to move, it has to be *now,*" Tray said.

"You just got away from her," Kenth pointed out. He felt like Tray was someone new, someone he'd never known, with his laughing face shadowed by memories of pain. How much had Kenth missed, being away? Would he have been able to protect his younger brother if he'd actually been here?

"We know firsthand why our niece can't be left to her. If she's a dragon—" Tray seemed to choke and he and Leinani exchanged a long, wordless exchange that Kenth felt awkward witnessing before they both turned back to him with their chins set. After a moment, Tray stepped forward and exchanged a swift embrace with Kenth.

"Fask said there would be no backup if I went," Kenth warned them. "Even three dragons…"

"Four," Rian corrected as he came in the side entrance and closed the distance to the tiny rebellion. "I already talked to Tania. She knew I'd need to come, too, to keep you fools from doing something dumb. But if you say one word about a matched pair, I'm out." He punched Tray, his twin, lightly in the arm and settled back on his heels. "Welcome home, Kenth, in case I didn't mention that before."

Kenth gave him an impulsive hug, then looked past him, to where three more figures were coming into the hall from the far entrance.

"I can get a jet to save us the flight there!" Toren called as he bounded across the ballroom. "Being Crown Prince comes with all kinds of privileges. All I have to do is call the airport and have them get it ready. No one even asks questions." Kenth wondered how much he'd really grown up after all; he looked like he was getting ready to go on a vacation, not on a dangerous rescue mission. He wasn't bothering to keep his voice down at all.

Raval followed more sedately. "I hope this doesn't take long," he groused. "I've got a project I'd rather be working on." He gave Kenth a crooked half-smile. "But you're our brother and she's our niece, and we'll back you."

Kenth saved his most skeptical look for the last figure, Drayger, the bastard prince from Majorca. "These guys have blood to blame," he pointed out. "What's your story?"

"I am *so bored,*" Drayger drawled with a cheeky grin. "I thought Alaska was going to be exciting when I defected here, but it's been nothing but yawns and dogs and a whole lot of snow since I got here. There is only so much hockey I can play before I go completely stir crazy."

"Captain Luke is going to put your head on a spike," Toren warned him. "She's already looking for a reason to throw you in the dungeon."

Drayger gave him a flashing smile. "I can give her all kinds of better reasons to do *that.*"

Kenth had to chuckle. "You guys do realize this is a mutiny, don't you? Fask is going to spit nails when he finds out what we've done." He sobered. "Seriously, are you sure? I have no right to ask for your help. I left this family five years ago and…you owe me nothing."

"We're not helping you because we owe you something," Rian said sensibly. "We're helping you because you're still our brother."

"It's the right thing to do," Toren said firmly. "Those poor kids."

"I have a debt to settle," Tray said, with uncharacteristic steel in his voice.

Leinani corrected, "*We* have a debt to settle."

"It seems more logical than waiting," Raval said with a

shrug. "We can't know that we'll ever have a better chance."

"It sounds like fun?" Drayger suggested playfully. "Besides, you're going to need some extra claws for all of those kids if we're breaking them out as dragons."

"We're going to have more of a plan, though, right?" Toren wanted to know. "They'll have guns, and magic, and more people."

"I like the odds of seven dragons against an honor guard," Drayger said. "Even if five of them are coddled *Alaskan* dragons." He winked at Leinani. "I can show you how dragons are *supposed* to fight."

Leinani raised one eyebrow at him, unamused. "They have tools to control dragons," she reminded them grimly, touching her neck.

"We'll have the element of surprise," Tray said grimly. "And Amara doesn't have our dragons to power her magic spells indefinitely anymore."

"She does still have some enchantments," Leinani cautioned. "We don't know what those magical guns will do."

"The one I shot didn't work at all," Tray pointed out.

"On Mackenzie," Leinani reminded him. "But she's immune to magic. We aren't."

Kenth felt Mackenzie before she was even in the doorway, the hesitant flutter of her presence just out of sight, and he left his brothers plotting strategy to meet her halfway across the great hall as if she'd drawn him to her on a fishing line.

"You're going to go after Dalaya anyway, aren't you?" she asked in a low voice when they were standing close together. "I want to go with you."

Kenth's instinct was to leave her here. She was a

human. An injured human, and his *mate*. She would be safest here, behind the protections of the Alaskan castle.

But he could see straight into her soul and see how well that would work.

"I have no hope of keeping you here where you'll be safe," he said with a sigh.

"Those kids trust *me*," Mackenzie said, her voice even though Kenth could feel her tremor of fear. "And I know how Amara's systems work. I can *help* you." She was the bravest thing that he had ever witnessed and he realized that no one else would ever guess it of her, because no one else would know how frightened and alone she felt. They would only see her quiet and docile front and not feel the resolve that was behind it.

"Mackenzie…"

"I can tell what spells will do before they are cast, and I can trip magical traps without endangering myself. I won't slow you down."

"Mackenzie…" It was hard to think around his overwhelming desire to simply sweep her up in his arms and kiss her. She was his, and he loved her, or would love her, and his dragon was as emotionally invested in her as he was.

"I need to do this," she said desperately.

"I won't stop you," Kenth said. "Toren is going to arrange a jet. Do you need to get anything?"

She looked at him with surprise and relief. "I don't have anything."

But she did, because she had his entire heart.

CHAPTER 5

It was the second time in as many days that Mackenzie had been on a fancy jet, and she was no more comfortable on this trip than she had been when she was with only Leinani and Tray. Most of her travel with the cult had been by ground when she was young, and later by portal because Amara wanted to keep her close.

A stewardess pointed her to a seat next to Kenth, who had shaved while their flight was being arranged and managed to look even more devastatingly beautiful and about ten years younger without a beard. He still had long, shaggy hair, but looked more like a book cover than a castaway now.

She shook her head when the stewardess offered a drink, but accepted a cookie—surprisingly warm—and then thought it was a mistake when she caught herself licking the melted chocolate off her fingers automatically. She saw Kenth glance at her the same moment she realized what she was doing and they exchanged a slow smile that warmed her more than the food before she remembered who he was.

It all seemed deeply unreal.

A prince.

She was sitting next to a dragon-shifting prince of Alaska who thought she was his mate. Mackenzie's smile slipped as she grappled with the idea. She wanted it to be true so badly that she wondered if she had somehow willed it into being. He was everything she had ever imagined: tall, broad-shouldered, good-looking, and protective.

Could he actually love her?

"Would you like another cookie?" he offered. He had a gorgeous grin when he wasn't storming around, breaking chairs into pieces, and without the beard to hide it, he had a magnificent jaw and an expressive mouth.

Mackenzie smiled back rather helplessly and shook her head, wiping the rest of the chocolate off of her hand more decorously with her napkin. Leinani, sitting across from them with Tray, was eating her cookie with perfect manners. She had probably never licked her fingers in her life.

Tray and Leinani were talking quietly; there was a wide space and a low table between the banks of couches, so it was easier to converse with Kenth than try to shout over the drone of the airplane engines.

"We didn't get a lot of cookies in the Cause," she said lightly, unable to think of anything else to say. It was nice that she didn't have to look at him as they spoke because they were sitting side-by-side. She was braver when she didn't have to see him, and less distracted by how handsome he was.

"Do you mind if I ask you questions about it?" Kenth asked, after a brief moment.

"I'm happy to answer anything I know. But like I said, Amara didn't trust me with a lot. She didn't trust anyone. I don't know how much help I can be."

"I don't mean about tactics or defenses or anything like that," Kenth hastened to clarify. "I mean, what was it like in the Cause. Did you grow up there? Were there other kids?"

"Oh," Mackenzie said in surprise. He cared?

"You don't have to say if you don't want," Kenth said firmly. Mackenzie snuck a sideways look at him. Did he sound angry? Frustrated? It really would be easier if she could tell what he felt, too.

"No, it's all right," Mackenzie said. "I don't remember an awful lot of my childhood, but there were no other kids until Amara got the focus stone. My mother was one of her followers and she died gloriously for The Cause when I was very young. I don't remember her at all. Amara was *generous* enough to raise me herself."

Did she sound as bitter as she felt? Did her voice matter when Kenth could collect her emotions straight out of her head?

"I realized my gift when we were squatting in this old, old farmhouse in northern Russia. I was probably eight. Amara had a spell on a carved piece of jade that she'd gotten in a black market, an enchantment that would make her words compelling. At this time, The Cause was all about how evil magic was, how we had to stop it from corrupting the world. Later, her message was seamlessly changed to how only *she* should have magic and we—they—stopped destroying artifacts and started collecting them."

"She couldn't figure out how to activate it or what it really did, but I looked at it and told her all of its tricks. From that moment on, I was really *important*. I could read any spell and tell her how to make it work. I could find them in old books and recognize them in pictures. I went from a bothersome orphan underfoot to Amara's favored hand."

"That was, what, ten years ago?"

"Fifteen." Mackenzie knew that she looked younger than she was. Kenth was older than her, she guessed, looking sideways at his profile, by maybe seven or eight years. She'd thought he was ten or fifteen years older with the beard.

"How did you…stay independent?"

"You mean, how did I avoid being brainwashed by Amara's persistent and pervasive propaganda?" Mackenzie licked her lips, tasting grief. "It helped that Amara relied more and more on magic to enchant her followers, and that doesn't work on me. But also, I read. I read desperately. Amara wanted me to research magic for her, find new spells to steal, and she thought I had to learn languages in order to understand them, so I had a language tutor and the freedom to go to libraries, both for study and to snoop for spells in old books."

Even just thinking about a library made her feel better. "I was so hungry for books that I taught myself to speed-read. I could go through a few novels in a morning if I focused, and I would do just enough study to bring Amara some new information every few days and spend the rest of the time absorbing everything that I could. Classics, at first, and history, but the librarians would smuggle me popular novels, young adult, fantasy, ah, romance."

Did he feel the rush of desire that came with that confession? Mackenzie plowed on. "I had to be careful about asking questions and making obvious requests, because there was usually a guard making sure that I didn't wander out into the modern world accidentally. I wasn't allowed to read newspapers or magazines. Fortunately, they weren't usually terribly literate themselves, so they didn't really *understand* how much I was consuming, or what it was. Books were books, to them."

"I used to put comic books inside my history books," Kenth said with a kind chuckle. "Look how studious I am!"

"They didn't allow you to read comic books?" Mackenzie asked seriously.

Kenth looked at her like he suspected a joke. "Not when I was supposed to be reading history."

It was weird to think that Mackenzie might have something in common with a prince, but she had to give a little laugh at his droll way of saying it. "Were you a terror to your tutors?" she guessed.

"Terror doesn't begin to describe it," Kenth laughed, then sobered. "I imagine that after a while, you were able to see through Amara's fiction."

"Her lies became obvious very quickly, but I was savvy enough not to let on to her that I was wavering in my loyalty. As far as she knew, I was only reading ancient history and still believed all the rhetoric that she taught. It helped that everyone around us was basically brainwashed, mostly by magic, and she never actually asked me what I was thinking. She knew that magic didn't work on me, but I don't think she really *thought* about the fact that she wasn't continuing to indoctrinate me when it worked so well on everyone else. She got sloppy and I knew better than to do anything out of line. I sat down when I was told, recited the creeds, and was quiet and obedient."

They sat in silence for a while, and Mackenzie wistfully asked, "What was your childhood like? What was it like to grow up...normally?" She'd read so much about the world, but knew so little about it.

Kenth turned to look at her and she accidentally met his gaze again. "I wouldn't know. I always wished I had grown up normally," he confessed. "Just another kid, going to school, playing computer games...maybe even dating."

"Not a prince?"

"Not a prince, not a dragon, not famous. I wanted to be able to compete in sports and go places without people snapping photographs. I wanted to be...ordinary."

"Yes," Mackenzie said breathlessly because she knew that feeling so well. "Yes, I understand that." She'd give anything to have a simple, ordinary life where she didn't have to always pretend to be something she wasn't. She wanted television and radio and bicycles, things that everyone thought were commonplace, but she'd never seen. She wanted the world she read about in books, where big problems were *does the boy like me* and *how do I win over mean girls*, not *who will get hurt* and *will I lose a little more of myself today*.

Kenth looked at her in wonder. "You really do," he said. "I mean, you get that. I tell my brothers and they just look at me blankly or ask why I want to be poor."

"It's not about being poor," Mackenzie agreed. "It's about being a whole person and not just an *expectation*. That's why you left Fairbanks," she guessed. "To give Dalaya a chance at that."

For a weird moment, Mackenzie thought Kenth was going to kiss her. His face was full of happiness, happiness that *she* had caused by understanding him.

"Thank you," he said after a moment.

"For what?"

"For getting me," he said simply.

He still looked like he wanted to touch her, which was an exciting and terrifying prospect. Touch had been a tool to Amara, hugs and affection always on her terms, withheld for displeasure and doled out to her whim. But Mackenzie knew it could be more, and she had read enough romance to wonder what it might be like to have Kenth touch her, to have his fingers on her bare skin.

Mackenzie had to fight to keep her imagination from

running away from her as she reminded herself firmly that he would know what she was feeling.

If her foolish heart didn't betray what she was thinking, her heated cheeks probably would. Fortunately, the cabin of the plane was dim.

Across from them, Tray and Leinani had fallen asleep leaning against each other, and Tray gave a little snore as he shifted in his seat and pulled Leinani closer.

"We should probably try to get some sleep, too," Kenth advised, demonstrating how to tip back his chair and accepting a pillow from a stewardess who suddenly appeared. "We're crossing some time zones and we'll want to act quickly once we get there. Who knows how much time we've actually got before Amara figures out the ring and moves on."

Mackenzie took a pillow, leaned her chair back, and closed her eyes, but it didn't help her feel restful.

He was so close, filling up the seat next to her, and so... Mackenzie almost giggled because the word that came to mind was *manly*. She wasn't in a work of literature; she was in a tawdry romance, and he was the shirtless highland prince from the most shameless paperback cover. *Does Alaska have a highland?* she wondered.

She was punch drunk, she realized. Too much had happened too quickly, and she was on the brink of bursting into hysterical tears. It was easier to think about the gorgeous guy beside her than all the uncertainty of where they were going, what she was trying to do.

She heard Kenth stir beside her and even as she tried to restrain her emotions to spare him her silly, irrational weakness, he reached out and found her hand in the darkness.

His fingers around hers were gentle and sure, just firm

enough to feel protected, but soft enough that she could pull away if she wanted.

It was the most perfect feeling that Mackenzie could imagine, an anchor of safety and comfort, and she clung to him, feeling all of her tension ease.

She didn't sleep, but he eventually did, and Mackenzie continued to gratefully hold onto his hand even when it went lax.

CHAPTER 6

*K*enth came awake with an ungraceful snort and realized that he was drooling on his pillow and still holding Mackenzie's hand.

She didn't seem to mind.

Indeed, she felt calmer and more resolved than ever. How much courage did it take to turn against everything she'd ever known?

"The stewardess said we'd be landing in about thirty minutes," she told him quietly.

Kenth slowly retrieved his hand, put his chair back up, and stretched. The cabin lights were back up and he had a crook in his neck from sleeping awkwardly, but he felt rested. Then he remembered that he was about to find the woman who had kidnapped his daughter, and all of his anger and outrage crowded back with a vengeance.

Across from them, Tray and Leinani were also waking up, rolling their shoulders. They were unashamed about holding hands and cuddling close to each other for comfort.

"We've had a bit of a war meeting in the back," Toren

said, slipping into the seat across the aisle. "We're talking about what we're going to do when we land. The hotel is on an island all the way over off the other side of the mainland and to travel there by surface would probably take a few hours and a boat. It would certainly be easiest to fly, but…"

"I can carry Mackenzie."

"It wouldn't be my first time," Mackenzie exchanged a wry look with Leinani.

"I feel I should apologize," the princess said, which was diplomatic but not exactly an apology.

Mackenzie shook her head. "It was better than what would have happened to me if you'd left me there." She looked at Kenth and hesitantly asked, "Can I…ride you?"

Toren gave an amused snort, and both Tray and Leinani smothered their own laughter.

Mackenzie looked from one to the other, not understanding the joke.

"You could," Kenth said, with a quelling general glare. "But it's not as easy as it sounds, and it can be dangerous if there is wind. The safer method of transportation would be in my claws."

"That's what she said," Toren chortled and Kenth might have reached across the aisle and decked him, but Mackenzie was only puzzled by the pop culture reference and not offended, though she was still trying to throttle her own chagrin.

"Seriously, though," Toren said when he had control of himself again. "Fask read me the riot act for taking Carina up in a familiar sheltered valley in fair weather. This would be a lot harder, and it's possible we might meet…resistance."

"Drayger suggested that he approach the compound by himself first because they shouldn't recognize him," Rian said, coming up the aisle to step past Toren into the next seat. Drayger was behind him. "What kind of cover story might help him get in, Mackenzie?"

Mackenzie frowned. "He might be able to say that he was part of the Dusk Cause. They're a group of Amara's influencers. Maybe a story about how he's been found out and is fleeing for his life? Do you know much about computers or social media?"

Drayger slipped past Kenth to settle in the seat past Mackenzie. "I can browse porno with the best of them," he joked.

Kenth glared at him and squashed his urge to pull Mackenzie away from him protectively. "I don't think that Drayger makes a very convincing cultist. Doesn't Amara know who they all are?"

"It's doubtful she's personally met all of them," Mackenzie said hesitantly, looking between them. "Especially her remote agents. It...could work."

"I don't see why we don't just attack the compound and take what we want by force," Kenth said. "There are seven of us—" should he count Mackenzie? he wondered belatedly.

"It doesn't seem sensible to pick a fight if maybe we don't have to," Toren said, chewing his lip in a completely not-kingly way.

"What do you think is going to happen when Drayger gets in?" Kenth snapped. "They're just going to give him Dalaya and all the other kids because he asks nicely?"

"I can be charming," Drayger said drolly. "But probably not that charming."

"He could at least get an idea of how many guards there are, what kind of protections they have," Rian pointed out. "We wouldn't be going in blind, then."

They were still arguing when the plane landed at a

small, private airfield, and still arguing as they disembarked and walked down the airstrip out of view.

Kenth walked beside Mackenzie, only remembering at the last moment not to take her hand, and didn't realize that they were doing anything odd until she looked behind them in confusion. "Won't they think this is…weird?"

Kenth shrugged. "There are only a few people here. They see a jet full of eccentric rich royal tourists hiking off to explore the wilds of an exotic island. They won't notice us as dragons."

"Because you naturally cloak," Mackenzie said thoughtfully. "A useful trick."

Kenth thought to wonder, "Are you immune to natural magic, too?" Spells and artifacts were part of structured magic and anyone could use them with the correct words, but shifting and cloaking were talents that someone was born with, less rigid and more innate.

Mackenzie nodded. "I'll be able to see you," she said confidentially.

Somehow, that seemed fitting, because she was already the person who saw him best. Or would be. Kenth shook his head to try to make sense of what he was feeling, then shunted it all aside. Most critical right now was saving Dalaya.

The terrain beneath them was rising steeply as Rian, with his GPS, led them unerringly away from the airstrip. The ground was gloriously green, and the sky was heavy and slate gray with cloud cover. It was a little like the tapestry of the earth had sucked all the colors from above, taking every hue for itself. There was snow at the tops of the ridges, making them fade into the sky.

"Let's go, then," Rian said, tucking away his phone and shivering into his dragon form. He bobbed his head and then leaped upwards, the backwash of his wing-strokes tossing Kenth's hair annoyingly. He was going to have to get a haircut when he got back to the castle. Assuming Fask didn't try to toss him directly out when he returned.

He hadn't really thought about returning to Alaska, too focused on the immediate goal of getting his daughter back. He glanced at Mackenzie, who was watching Rian spiral up into the sky with awe in her face. Would she stay with him, once her own mission concluded? He could not doubt the strength of their possible future, but it might be that she would reject her role in it.

Having a mate was supposed to eliminate a need for courtship and skip right to the happy ever after, but if she didn't feel the bond...Kenth suddenly doubted his ability to win her. Would she *want* to return to a tiny town at the end of a road with him and Dalaya? Would she prefer a life of state in Fairbanks? Would she want to be with him at all? She had a whole world to explore now. What did a grouch like him have to offer her?

We are enough, his dragon said contentedly.

Kenth wished he had the same confidence.

Four more dragons flowed up after Rian, leaving Kenth and Mackenzie alone on the heather as they circled overhead.

"Are you ready?" he asked gently.

She nodded crisply, and because Kenth could feel her fear and misgiving, he could see little hints of it in her serene face. He guessed that she was remembering her last, terrifying trip by dragon, and he could feel her side ache.

Kenth wasn't sure what to say to reassure her, so he stepped back and said nothing, instead shifting into his dragon form.

His dragon always gave a little sigh of relief when they shifted, like he was coming out of a box that was too small, and Kenth spread his wings wide and stretched from his nose to the tip of his tail.

Mackenzie seemed tiny from his new vantage, and she bravely held her ground when Kenth closed the distance between them and offered her one of his front claws.

She licked her lips and stepped up onto him, holding onto a claw as he folded the others gently around her. She was tall enough that he held her at the waist as she stood in his claws, like a cage of talons around her. Kenth turned, careful to keep his forearm as still as he could, leaned back, and sprang up on his strong back legs, beating his wings as he went.

Mackenzie was not heavy, but he was hyper-aware of her clinging to him. Her terror slowly eased into awe as Kenth climbed up above the spine of the island and banked to follow the dragons ranged in the sky before him.

The clouds were low over the steep, volcanic hills, and the islands were jagged green jewels over a wrinkled blue-green sea. There was snow at the peaks.

Kenth flew over half a dozen of the islands, trusting Rian's map memory to take them to the hotel where Amara must be. He didn't let himself wonder if Leinani's ring had led them true. It was his only lead to Dalaya.

The hotel was alone, a cluster of buildings high on one slope of the island, a narrow winding road leading to it before it went on to a tiny fishing town on the bay below. It did not look particularly defensible as they flew overhead, investigating the best way to land and approach.

The terrain was like a carelessly dropped linen napkin, sharply draped and full of crevices and canyons. Kenth picked a sheltered spot closest to the hotel itself and led the dragons down to it. Drayger alone peeled off and chose the road that approached it, clearly intent on following the original plan and walking up to the front door directly.

"Can you see the spells from here?" he asked Mackenzie as she stepped from his grip and he shifted to human.

The others took turns landing and shifting beside him, and Mackenzie shook her head regretfully. "I'm too far away to see them."

They had a view of the hotel from behind and above and could see part of the road beyond it. Drayger was already approaching on foot, a careless swagger to his pace.

Toren had thought to bring binoculars and he reported, "There are guards along the roof. He's got their attention."

Most of the buildings on the island had peaked roofs, but this hotel had clearly been built to foreign franchise specifications; it looked like a generic motel and had four stories facing the ocean view. The town was around another one of those rock wrinkles and the stunning view was all ocean and tiny volcanic islands.

"This is definitely the sort of place Amara prefers," Mackenzie said, peering down at it.

"She's got a type," Tray said dryly. "Seedy motel, off by themselves."

"How long do we wait?" Leinani asked. "There are more guards now."

"This isn't going to work," Kenth said flatly. "No one in their mind is going to think Drayger is a cultist."

"He'll call," Toren said optimistically.

"Only if they let him keep his phone," Kenth pointed out.

On cue, Rian's phone rang.

He put it on speakerphone and held it out between them. "Dray—?"

"I don't know how that got there," Drayger's voice protested distantly. "How mysterious."

Kenth reached out and hung up. "Gig's up," he said firmly. He turned to Mackenzie. "Stay here, stay safe. We're doing this my way now."

Allowing no further argument, he shifted and surged up into the sky, flying straight for the hotel and his daughter.

He heard Toren protest behind him, "This is not a plan! This is the opposite of a plan! What are you doing?!"

CHAPTER 7

The brothers swore colorfully, and even Leinani even said, "Dammit!" but not one of them remained behind as Kenth led the ill-conceived charge directly on the hotel itself.

Mackenzie was left quite alone, standing on the ridge looking down at the swath of destruction they left as they took the fight to the guards on the flat rooftop and circled to flame at the front door.

There was gunfire, and Mackenzie reminded herself that Amara's men wouldn't be able to see the dragons, only shimmers of motion at the corners of their eyes and the fire that they blazed. That didn't mean that they wouldn't make some lucky shots, and although she knew from her own escape that dragons had thick, armored hide, *enough* bullets could bring them down.

She wished she was the kind of person to stand up and yell at Kenth for being a complete idiot, but he wouldn't be able to hear her…and she wasn't going to do any good up here waiting for them all to come back.

It was a hard scramble down the scree of the slope, and

Mackenzie had to trust that everyone was staying busy in the fight as she crept through the short heather, taking what shelter there was in the storage sheds and broken equipment behind the abandoned hotel.

The bottom windows of the hotel had all been enspelled to ward away any intruders, but Mackenzie felt the magic slip off of her like oil, and she smashed in the first window with a large landscaping rock. She waited, listening for an alarm from someone who might have heard her, then broke away the shards and crawled into the building.

The window opened into a daylight basement and she had to drop blindly to the dark floor, trusting that it wasn't too far. She hit before she expected to, and the impact jarred her side and reminded her that it hadn't been terribly long since she'd been stabbed in the ribs.

She got her balance and glanced back up. She wasn't sure how she'd get out now that she was in, but she'd cross that bridge when she got to it. Maybe the princes would defeat Amara's forces and they could all just walk out the front door. She laughed dryly at herself for her ridiculous optimism.

But ridiculous optimism had gotten her this far.

The room she was in was empty and dusty, and the door opened out onto a quiet hallway. She could hear pounding footsteps stories above her, and more explosions outside. Quiet as a mouse, she slipped in a random direction. Amara tended to keep valuable hostages near her. If Kenth's daughter was here, she would be at the top level... with the rest of Mackenzie's goal.

She found a stairwell and winced at the shrieking creak that the fire door gave as she slipped in. But no one seemed to respond to it, so she bounded up the stairs.

As she passed the third floor for the fourth, a door

beneath her smashed open. Mackenzie backed into the wall and pressed herself against it, trying to decide whether to risk running up or staying silent. If they came up, there was nowhere to hide, and no shelter. Magic wouldn't stop her, but bullets would, and she did not for a moment assume that anyone had memories of her that would be stronger than Amara's influence spells. Voices shouted and cultists clambered down a level on noisy stairs, the door crashing closed behind them.

Mackenzie crept up the final floor. The noise from the roof above covered the creak of the door as she opened it.

This was a more well-appointed space, with carpeted halls and big windows at each end.

There were people on this floor. Mackenzie could hear voices from open doors. More of them were on the roof, she thought, and all of the sounds of battle seemed to be on one side of the building. Hopefully, the prize she was after was on the other side.

Here, however, she was thwarted because all of the doors she tried were locked. She couldn't know who was on the other side, didn't have a key. Could she find Amara's room and steal a master key? Was there a housekeeping cart she could raid?

Finally, Mackenzie screwed up her nerve and knocked on each door, a careful shave-and-a-haircut count.

Most of the doors were silent. A gruff "What was that?" answered one and Mackenzie fled and hid in the next door alcove until she was convinced that she wouldn't be pursued.

And at the fifth one, she got lucky.

"Who is it?" a young voice demanded. A familiar voice.

"It's Mackenzie," she said, as loud as she dared.

The door opened wide and she slipped inside at the sound of raised voices further down the hall.

"Mackenzie!"

Children in the cult were never encouraged to be affectionate, so Mackenzie was surprised when Elijah impulsively stepped forward and embraced her. "Amara said you'd gone away forever, that you didn't like us anymore."

Mackenzie squeezed him back. He was as tall as her collarbone now, and that always surprised her. Behind her, the rest of the kids had drawn to obedient attention and were frozen suspiciously in place. They all looked distressed and exhausted, and Mackenzie was furious for the strain that showed in their faces. She could tell that Amara had been driving them too hard. Would she have time to destroy the stone before they left so that this could never happen again?

One little girl stood out among them, not only because she was half the age of the next-youngest child and a stranger, but because she was still sitting with her arms crossed, looking defiant and suspicious, not nearly as subdued as the others. Dark waves framed her frowning face.

This had to be Dalaya; Mackenzie could see Kenth's stubborn scowl even in her chubby cheeks and soft mouth.

"I came to get you," she said, stepping out of Elijah's embrace to circle the room. Amara hadn't set up any protections here, trusting her magical conditioning to work on them. Mackenzie had deliberately never told her how quickly it faded on young minds, and the cult leader was used to the effect it had on her adult followers. "We have to go now, while we can."

"The demons are attacking," one of the other children said hesitantly.

"Remember the stories I told you about demons being

good people under a spell?" Mackenzie said coaxingly. "Remember the stories about nice people who would take us all home?"

"There would be hot cocoa," Cindy, a girl of about ten, said wistfully. "And everyone gets their own pillow."

"We can have that now," Mackenzie said, "but we have to go, quickly and quietly." She was standing before Dalaya now, and Dalaya looked like she was going to cry or pitch a fit and was only trying to decide which.

"Hi, Dalaya, I'm Mackenzie. I...know your dad." It would have been more accurate to say that her dad knew Mackenzie, she thought wryly, since he was the only one who actually felt their hypothetical bond. But explaining mates—especially *broken* mates—to a five-year-old seemed like a poor use of short time.

"Menzie," Dalaya repeated warily. Her face had brightened a tiny bit at the word *dad*.

The rest of the children looked perilously unconvinced. "Leader Amara says they're bad," one said slowly.

"I don't want to go," another whined.

"I'm tired."

Mackenzie gritted her teeth. "In a line, now," she commanded. "We don't have time." She almost added automatically, *The Cause calls you*, but stopped herself before she did. The children shuffled wearily into formation anyway.

Mackenzie offered Dalaya her hand. "Let's get you back to your daddy." Dalaya bounced eagerly up and put her little hand trustingly in Mackenzie's.

Randal was at the end of the line. "Mackenzie," he said in his nasal voice. "Mackenzie went away." The oldest of the children by a wide margin, he was slow to speak and slow to think. That was the only reason that the stone still worked on him, at his age.

"I came back for you, Randal," Mackenzie told him. She squeezed his shoulder, and he stared at her in his unsettling fashion. Then he gave her a scrunched-up half-smile that showed a lot of teeth.

She listened at the door before she opened it, chewing on her lip and concentrating on the voices before she dared to look out. There were guards clustered near the stairwell at one end of the hallway. The sounds of the overhead battle had stopped, and in the silence after the gunfire, she could hear the sound of dragons landing on the roof, making it creak with their weight. All of their activity was at one end of the building.

Did she dare try to sneak all of the kids out the other end, hoping that they kept attention away from their escape? She wracked her brain for any other choice.

She hadn't come all this way to fail now.

CHAPTER 8

Kenth knew where Mackenzie was. It wasn't as accurate as a GPS tracker, but he knew her general direction and could tell when she got to the top floor. He and his brothers cleared the roof and landed there, taking what cover there was from the mechanical equipment there before they shifted.

"We are never going to get down that stairwell in one piece," Toren said. "There's just too many of them."

"We can't exactly go in as dragons," Rian said practically. "And we don't have that much of an advantage in a fight as humans. They're armed to the teeth, and there are only seven of us."

"Out here in the air is one thing," Tray agreed with uncharacteristic grimness. "I don't know how you expect to get in."

"I'm not just leaving my daughter and my mate with her," Kenth snarled, but he could feel the despair in his chest. They were hopelessly outnumbered and had no tactical power.

"Wait, Mackenzie's in there?" Leinani asked in surprise. "She was supposed to wait outside."

"She got in while we were busy," Kenth said. He pointed halfway down the roof. "She's there, top floor. She found them. I felt it. But she doesn't know how to get out now." Her relief at finding them had been clear, but so was her helplessness now.

Raval looked thoughtfully down the length of the building. "Can you have her meet us at the end of the building at the fire escape?"

Kenth shook his head in frustration. "I don't have any way to communicate with her. It's not as convenient as a two-way radio."

"Can she hear us through the roof?" Rian asked. "Could we tap Morse code to her?"

Kenth walked to the edge of the roof and looked down. "Maybe we make our own fire escape," he hissed. He raised his arms and shifted as he jumped, rising up into the sky on strong wings.

"This is still not a plan!" Toren called in outrage after him, but when Kenth glanced back, Toren had already shimmered into his dragon form and was spreading his own wings.

Kenth didn't wait to see if the others would follow, but only drove higher and higher up into the sky before turning to dive back at full speed, straight for the room where he knew Mackenzie was hiding.

His brothers scattered aside at his arrow-straight approach and at the last moment, Kenth folded his wings, curled himself in, and hit the side of the building like a cannonball.

The impact knocked all of the wind out of him, but the wall cracked and broke in, both windows shattering.

Blind for a moment and disoriented, Kenth was

battered by Mackenzie's shock and fear, then her wave of relief when she recognized him. He was more out of the building than in it and had to scrabble with claws and outspread wings when gravity overcame momentum and he threatened to fall. Chunks of wall tore away from his slashing talons until he could see into the room and hold on to the exposed steel structure.

Dust and crumbled ceiling panels clouded the scene, but he found Mackenzie at once, and his heart filled with hope when he saw that Dalaya was pressed up tight against her…along with almost a dozen other children of various ages and stages of terror. Pieces of ceiling panel were falling and Kenth hadn't hit the building quite where he meant to; part of the floor was missing where he'd struck the structure between floors instead of simply punching through the wall.

Another dragon joined him in clawing at the opening in the wall, Tray, and after only a moment, the graceful form of Leinani, the two of them working in careful tandem to widen the escape route.

"Don't be afraid!" Mackenzie was shouting. For a moment, Kenth was confused, because she moved to the door. But she wasn't trying to escape; she was getting behind the children to herd them away from it and throw the deadbolt, and not a moment too soon. There was the sound of pounding on the other side of it, and then a muffled explosion. Amara was not going to lose her prizes without a fight.

"Don't be afraid!" Mackenzie repeated. "They are here to help us! Stay together, I've got you!" They clung to her, weeping and screaming, and she waded with them bravely for the broken wall. She handed Dalaya over first, and Kenth was glad when the little girl scrambled into his outstretched claw. She was used to his dragon form and didn't fear it, even though he could tell from her trembling that she was afraid. The other children stared, but Dalaya's trust and Mackenzie's unending assurances seemed to do the job. One stepped onto Tray's outstretched claw, two more together into Leinani's. Kenth coaxed Dalaya over to Tray's free claw and was glad to see his brother flee with Leinani, freeing space for other dragons at the broken side of the building. Toren took three of the smallest, tucking them—sobbing but brave—into his foreclaws before kicking off and fleeing after Tray and Leinani.

Drayger dropped from above, clacking his amusement or disapproval—Kenth wasn't sure which—and took two of the trembling children in his claws. Raval took two, stoic and expressionless even as a dragon.

At last, only Mackenzie remained, and one teenager, who was curled in a miserable ball at the far end of the ruined room near the door, rocking back and forth in distress.

Kenth growled, jerking his head at the diminishing forms of the dragons, getting the other children away while they could. He could hear troops taking the roof again, and he didn't want to risk getting Mackenzie shot at as they escaped. Their window of opportunity was rapidly closing.

"I'm not leaving him!" Mackenzie shouted.

Kenth roared in frustration even as he admired her loyalty, just as the doorway to the hall dissolved in an explosion. It knocked the boy and Mackenzie down together and sent them sliding across the room towards the missing wall.

In the smoking doorway stood a tall and furious woman who must be Amara, a crackling shield of energy around her and two guards with carved weapons flanking her. Mackenzie scrambled to her feet, dragging the boy with her, and ran for Kenth.

He didn't dare flame in Amara's direction for fear of hitting his mate or the child. As soon as the kid was within his reach, Kenth reached forward and snatched the boy into a clawed fist without waiting for him to climb sedately on.

One gun flashed and snapped a bolt of pure blue energy at Kenth, but before it could hit him, Mackenzie shot to her feet and intercepted it. It sizzled harmlessly around her, dissipating into nothing. The second gun flashed and she dived to try to block it, but the tiny shot went wide of her and buried itself in Kenth's shoulder.

He tensed for magical pain or paralysis, then heaved a hot breath of relief when it seemed to do no damage. Shots rained down from the roof overhead. Mackenzie ran for him and Kenth turned so that he was ready to launch as soon as she was in his reach. He had to grab her with his off-talon because the child was struggling in his best claw and he didn't want to risk dropping him. He gave a final flame to mask their flight and had both rear feet free to kick off from the building and spread wings, protecting them both with his body from the gunfire above.

For a moment, he feared he had overestimated his ability to carry both of them, dropping far faster than he should. His wings strained to lift them, creaking, and lucky shots tore through the membranes.

It wasn't enough to keep him from flight and then, at last, they were all away, and the shots and shouts faded beneath them as Kenth took to the sky, following his brothers with all the speed he could muster.

CHAPTER 9

Mackenzie decided she enjoyed traveling by dragon even less than she liked jets.

Kenth's claws were gentle around her, but they were still massive digits holding her basically sideways in a cage. She'd been upright on the trip from the airport, but Kenth hadn't had time to settle her correctly on their way back. The wind roaring past couldn't quite cut out Randal's panicked sobs from Kenth's other talons and she was tempted to join him in weeping. She had to shut her eyes against the biting wind and was dizzy and sick to her stomach. Her braid had come unwound and her hair whipped into her face and stuck in her mouth.

Her side hurt like fire, and her nerves were badly rattled. Had all the children safely escaped? Was Amara still pursuing them? Were there injuries?

Had she done the right thing, even attempting this crazy rescue?

They flew for longer than Mackenzie thought they could, high up over the spine of the island. Randal's sobbing eventually stopped, and she had a moment of feeling her stomach drop out. Then they were landing at the far end of the airstrip, Kenth releasing them at last.

The other children were already there, some distance away. Randal picked himself up and staggered over to them while Mackenzie knelt wearily on the airport asphalt and wondered if there was any part of her that didn't hurt. She had hair in her mouth, but it seemed like too much effort to get it out.

Then, to her alarm, the giant dragon that had carried them transformed back into Kenth and he bore down on her and gathered her, unprotesting, into his arms.

He held her like a drowning man, as if she'd been the one who just carried him to safety instead of the other way around, his face buried in her hair. "Mackenzie," he murmured.

If she felt the mate bond like he did, would this be right and familiar? Mackenzie was divided between thinking that his embrace was the most natural, perfect thing in the world and feeling like she was being manhandled by a complete stranger. She wanted to relax into those strong arms and she wanted to fight her way free, both at the same time. Indecision froze her, and after a moment, Kenth let go.

She immediately felt bereft and her shiver wasn't because she was cold.

"I'm sorry," he said, his voice thick. "I didn't mean to make you feel uncomfortable. It's hard to remember that you don't feel this. Now, at least."

"Daddy?"

Dalaya extricated herself from the others and dashed erratically towards them. Kenth knelt down and intercepted her, lifting her into the air and crushing her into a desperate hug. "Dalaya, my darling." He cupped the back of her head with a big hand, tangling fingers in her hair and he embraced her whole-heartedly, cuddling her close.

His tenderness and affection were amazing to witness. Mackenzie felt like she was watching something very intimate, something she'd never known to miss in her own life.

"I was brave!" Dalaya said. "They took me away and I cried and I missed you and I want to go home and I'm *tired.*" She lay her head trustingly on Kenth's shoulder and sobbed, utterly overwrought. Mackenzie found herself wanting to do the same.

She turned away instead, pulling hair from her mouth, trying to smooth it back from her wind-burned face, as the rest of the kids crowded around her.

"Where are we?" Cindy asked, tears welling in her eyes.

"What happens now?"

"I'm scared!"

"Mackenzie, I don't like this."

Mackenzie lifted her chin. "These are the people I told you about. The people who could help us."

"They're demons," Elijah said skeptically. "We saw."

Randal just wrapped his arms around himself and swayed in place.

"Kenth? Can we have a brief aside on the topic of what's next?" Rian called.

The other dragons, none of them looking more than vaguely ruffled, had gathered to one side, just beyond easy earshot.

Mackenzie's exclusion was clear.

She gathered the kids to her and gave the dragons space. There might have been activity far away down the little airfield, but there were no sounds of sirens. She glanced in the direction they'd come from, half-expecting to see pursuit in the sky, but there was none.

Mackenzie didn't have any answers to the questions that were rattled at her; she wasn't sure what would happen now. She'd never had a clear game plan beyond 'get the children out.'

She had no money or power, and she was not sure if she could call the dragon royalty friends. Certainly, they had been friendly, but how much of that was in self-interest? Mackenzie was under no illusions; if Kenth's daughter had not been one of Amara's captives, they would not have come.

Now she was not just an inconvenient cult castoff with very little valuable information, but she was also saddled with eleven children.

She didn't know how much being Kenth's mate would count for, or helping to rescue Tray and Leinani, measured against the annoyance that she was now.

The motion at the far end of the airfield resolved into a jet, motoring steadily towards them on the ground.

Mackenzie got the children lined up at the edge of the tarmac and was irrationally relieved when Kenth, still carrying an exhausted Dalaya, returned to her side and firmly assured her, "You don't have to worry anymore. About anything."

She reined in her concerns, mortified that she'd subjected him to all her doubts and fears after all that he'd already done for them. "I'm grateful for your help," she said honestly. *Don't feel, don't fumble, don't make waves. I am a good little pawn.*

Kenth cast her a concerned sideways look, and she wondered how much, exactly, he was picking up from her. She would have to ask him when she could.

Then the plane reached them, and she was too busy keeping the exhausted and overstimulated children in an orderly line to climb the narrow plane stairs.

CHAPTER 9 71

They seemed cautiously optimistic, and excited about dragons once they'd laid aside the idea of demons. There were some tears, Cindy had a hundred-yard stare, and Randal was stimming desperately, but for the most part, they trusted Mackenzie was taking them some place better, a place that she'd told them about in stories, a place where they wouldn't have nightmares of magic, where they could write without wondering what their words would do.

That was what mattered, not what happened to her. Mackenzie wearily climbed after them and helped get them all buckled in. They fell upon the offered cookies like animals and Mackenzie took the final empty seat, between Kenth, who had Dalaya in his lap, and Randal.

There was no opportunity for private conversation, but Kenth took her hand after a moment and Mackenzie felt much better for it. She might not have been ready for his unexpected embrace, but having his fingers touching hers felt as right as anything in the world ever had.

She fell asleep this time, dreamed of green knives in a purple sea cutting off her unexpected wings, and woke up with Randal curled awkwardly in her lap. Kenth's hand was no longer in hers; he was busy typing one-handed on his phone while Dalaya, asleep, occupied the other arm.

He glanced over and gave her a soft smile that Mackenzie thought might qualify as toe-curling; she'd always thought that descriptions in books were ridiculous, but she was reconsidering some of those assumptions. Her knees really did feel weak when he grinned at her, sometimes, and there really was a flutter in her stomach when she first caught sight of him each time. Maybe somewhat lower than her stomach.

"What happens now?" she asked quietly, trying to stretch what she could without disturbing Randal.

Kenth's smile faded, and he glowered at the phone.

"Well, as you can imagine, Fask is unhappy with this development." He glanced at her and hastened to add, "You aren't in trouble and don't have to worry about anything."

Mackenzie realized he must have felt her stab of panic at his words. "I don't want to be in the way," she said.

"You *aren't* in the way," Kenth said fiercely. He gentled his voice as both Dalaya and Randal stirred. "You are… our guest."

Mate.

Mackenzie knew what he wasn't saying.

She was his *mate*.

It must be such an embarrassment, she thought. She was a nobody. He was a prince. She was *worse* than a nobody, she was the Hand of their enemy. Why would he trust her? Why would he…want her?

Mackenzie thought fixedly of the children, of ensuring their safety and freedom, so that she wouldn't think about Kenth *wanting* her. That would mean she had to admit how much she was coming to want *him* and she had learned the hard way that wanting anything only gave people power over her.

"The kids?" she said, focusing her thoughts. "What happens to them now?"

Kenth's jaw tightened. "They're safe," he vowed. "We'll try to find their families and they will have whatever they need in the meantime. We'll hire Mary Poppins, if we have to, and set up a school in the throne room."

"You've read Mary Poppins?" Mackenzie stared at him.

"It's a book?" Kenth said in surprise. "I've only seen the movie."

"It's a whole series of books," Mackenzie said. Then she shyly added, "I've *never* seen a movie."

CHAPTER 9

The look that Kenth gave her was dismay and surprise. "Not a single movie?"

Mackenzie shook her head. "I haven't watched television, either. We weren't even allowed to listen to the radio."

She braced herself for pity, or perhaps anger on her behalf, and she was surprised when Kenth chuckled. "I'm almost jealous," he whispered to her.

Jealous? He was jealous of her? It must be a joke she didn't get.

"You'll see," he warned her. "The seventeenth rewatch of Little Tree Friends, and you'll wish you were back there. Keep your cookies and credit cards, you'll say, let me crawl back to Amara where I won't have to endure this cotton candy torture anymore."

He really was joking, Mackenzie realized, hesitantly smiling back. He was watching her carefully, like he wanted to make sure that the humor landed with her. "I'm teasing," he said frankly. "We'll watch every movie you want when we get home." He gave an exaggerated sigh. "Even Little Tree Friends, for the eighteenth time."

Mackenzie wondered which part of the statement was most astonishing. The idea of being teased in fun was delightful. She was longing to watch her first movie. But most of all, he'd said they were going *home*, and she didn't know what to do with that idea.

CHAPTER 10

Fask would have yelled a lot more if it hadn't been for the children, Kenth was sure.

They were remarkably well-behaved, and Kenth wasn't sure if it was because they had been trained to obedience, or if it was because they were so exhausted that they could barely walk. He remembered that they had only moved from Crete a few days before and that their rescue by "demons" must have been deeply traumatic. They slept on the plane, but only fitfully.

They clung around Mackenzie like a small herd of dazed goats now, and she led them swiftly through the cold from the limos up the grand front steps of the castle.

Mrs. James, the white-haired housekeeper who hadn't aged a day since Kenth had left, met them inside the door with a tray of hot chocolate, clucking over their state. "We're still preparing a suite for the girls and one for the boys," she said. "We couldn't arrange individual rooms, but everyone gets their own bed."

A little sepia-skinned girl took her cup of cocoa and said in wonder, "I get my own pillow?"

Mrs. James burst into tears.

Carina and Tania were there, handing out sweaters and stuffed animals. Kenth wasn't sure where it had all come from. He'd called in their arrival from the air with fairly minimal details, so Mrs. James must have had just enough time to coordinate a swift shopping trip. He wondered how the media was going to explain the royal family suddenly buying up carts of toys and children's clothing. It was bound to make the news.

Fask scowled plenty, even if he didn't yell, and drew Kenth aside, undoubtedly to scold him.

Kenth wasn't interested in letting Dalaya go and she chose to stay in his arms rather than get a cup of hot chocolate, though she watched the others with big, wondering eyes and gazed up around at the high, carved ceiling and all the artwork on the walls. Fask had redecorated, Kenth realized. It was all much more to Fask's taste than their father's now. Kenth wondered if he hated it because it was Fask's idea to change things or if he really missed their father's art.

"This is Dalaya," he said, to open the conversation. "Dalaya, this is your Uncle Fask."

"It's nice to meet you," Fask said rather awkwardly.

Dalaya was shy, hiding her face at Kenth's neck.

"She's had a big day," Kenth said, not forcing her to be social.

"You don't say," Fask snapped. "What with invading foreign soil and blowing up a building. How the hell am I supposed to explain this?"

"Explain what?" Kenth said with a shrug.

"A royal-registered Alaskan plane lands in the Faroe Islands. A hotel blows up. The royal Alaskan plane conveniently leaves immediately after. It's not like the dots are hard to put together. Are they going to come after us for

CHAPTER 10

kidnapping? There are going to be a lot of questions. Questions that *I'm* going to have to answer for."

"I did not blow up the hotel," Kenth scoffed. "I smashed one little hole in it."

"You were stupid and irresponsible!" Fask did yell then. "I told you not to go and we are all going to be lucky if we don't have a giant international incident over this mess."

"I'm sure you can go suck the right—" Kenth reconsidered his word at the last moment. "I'm sure you can smooth it all over with your very impressive diplomatic skills."

"I'm sure I will," Fask snarled. "You certainly won't."

Captain Luke waved Fask aside, her expression as neutral as always. Fask looked a little like he wanted to stay and argue more. Then he gave a noise of great disgust and stalked away.

Dalaya's weight was making Kenth's shoulder ache, and he remembered belatedly that he'd been shot there. It was a minor injury, not worth bringing any attention to; it hadn't even bled on his shirt when he shifted back into human form. Mrs. James and Mackenzie were fussing over the kids, putting bandages and ointment on scratches. Maybe he should let Mackenzie put one on him.

"Oh, Kenth," Mrs. James said, looking up to see him. "I've got you set up in your old rooms in the east wing. Dalaya is just across the sitting room from you, and Mackenzie will be just past her."

Mackenzie looked up at the sound of her name. "I, ah, I was in a room in the west wing last night."

"We made some adjustments, dear," Mrs. James said breezily. "We wanted you by the other children, of course. They trust you and this way, they'll be just down the hall from you. Your things are already moved and there are clean clothes for you laid out." It sounded innocent enough, but Kenth caught the edge of her wink at Mackenzie.

Mackenzie's chagrin rang in Kenth's head and she yanked her gaze away to busy herself with one of the girls' jacket zippers.

Kenth had to laugh, for the first time in what felt like a really long time, because he could tell that Mackenzie was embarrassed by the idea, but more intrigued than mortified. "Very subtle, Mrs. James," he told her quietly, pulling her into a one-armed embrace.

"We've missed you, Kenth," she said candidly. "Even if we didn't miss the fights. And you brought us a daughter!" She cooed at Dalaya, but Dalaya had clearly had enough of strangers and excitement and still had her face tucked firmly into his hair.

"I'll give you a haircut first thing tomorrow, Kenth," Mrs. James added with a cluck of disapproval. Then she was bustling off to help one of the children trying on a pair of boots.

Dalaya gave a sigh.

"You want to see your room, Darling Dalaya?" Kenth asked her.

"I'm not sleepy," she insisted into his neck.

"I bet you are," Kenth said teasingly.

"No," Dalaya said. "No, no, no, no, no."

She was still saying no, more and more weakly, when he tucked her into the big bed that Mrs. James had made up for her. He stayed beside her until she was completely asleep and then watched for a long while longer.

For years now, she had been his everything.

Watching her sleep, her mouth just parted, her eyelashes fanned over her cheek, Kenth felt like things were right again; losing her had been like having a limb cut off.

CHAPTER 10

And now she was back, and safe, and there was more in his heart than he'd ever dared to hope for.

Mackenzie.

She was like a bird, fluttering around in his ribcage. He could feel what they were going to be to each other, in a confusing swirl with all of her complicated emotions now and all her future feelings. He longed to go to her and bring her here where she belonged, here with Dalaya, to comfort her and convince her that everything had happened exactly as it was meant to.

His *mate.*

He had a mate and a daughter and a destiny and just that morning he'd thought he had nothing left in the world.

A lot could change in a day.

He tucked the blanket up around Dalaya's shoulder a little more snugly—she would knock it off by morning anyway—and laid a kiss on her forehead before retreating through the sitting room to his own bedroom.

His rooms had been turned into a generic guest suite; nothing personal remained. Probably they had boxed his things and hauled them down to the vault when he left. He'd taken little with him and never missed the rest. They lived a simple life in a tiny village and he didn't have a powerful urge to hoard things like his brothers did.

There was a clean change of clothes and a pair of pajamas out on the bed. Kenth weighed his exhaustion against the thought of climbing into a clean bed with his grimy body and decided a shower was worth the effort.

He caught a glimpse of his shoulder in the fogging bathroom mirror as he pulled his shirt off and paused to wipe away the steam and look closer.

The wound was closed, but stained black. Some kind

of poison? Kenth poked it. There was a strange, deep ache to it, but no surface pain at all.

He washed it in the shower, but the black discoloration didn't come up with vigorous soap or scrubbing.

Hurts, his dragon complained, but Kenth couldn't pinpoint where the pain actually was.

After he toweled off, he fell directly into bed, not bothering with pajamas.

CHAPTER 11

"I still cannot believe you were holding a niece out on us," Toren said to Kenth the next day at lunchtime. "You want the blue crayon, kiddo?"

"Yes, please!" Dalaya sang.

The enormous front hall had been set up as a temporary classroom with tables and chairs, and the liberated kids had been showered with new art supplies and toys and books while Fask, somewhat grudgingly, deployed the royal resources to find their true families. The staff doted on their new charges almost to the exclusion of the royal brothers.

"You are a grown man and can go make yourself a sandwich," Mrs. James told Kenth when they brought out lunch for the kids, to their great amusement. Each child got a custom-made plate with their favorite foods, and a sandwich bar had been laid out for everyone else in the informal dining hall. Kenth wasn't particularly hungry and hadn't wanted to leave Dalaya's side to fend for himself. He was loath to leave her alone for any amount of time after witnessing how sudden her abduction had been, even if he told himself that she could be no safer than here, surrounded by his family.

Fask was hiring new kitchen help, housekeepers, and a teacher for the kids, sighing with resignation and admitting that they were already strained with the influx of mates that the castle had recently seen. He had offered to retain a nanny specifically for Dalaya, but Kenth had firmly clarified that he was not interested in Fask's help with anything regarding his daughter.

She was drawing now, with the crayons and paper that had been provided at her seat.

"What a beautiful picture," Carina said enthusiastically. "Is it a house?"

"It's a sandwich," Dalaya said matter-of-factly. "Daddy is hungry, too."

"Thanks, kitten," Kenth said. "Yum, it's delicious."

"It's not finished," Dalaya admonished.

"Of course it's not," Carina agreed. "Really, Kenth, what were you thinking?" she teased.

Kenth liked Toren's mate. It was hard to imagine a better match for Toren's merry nature and energy. Likewise, Tania, the quiet woman who often walked with an ornate cane, seemed in every way Rian's perfect companion. They quoted obscure books at each other in a baffling second language, often having entire conversations that no one else could track.

Tray, to Kenth's surprise, had sobered considerably, probably a product of his month of imprisonment and torture. The perfectly deported Princess Leinani was a surprising match for him, but they seemed to be unexpectedly compatible and unflaggingly supportive of each other.

The boy across the table from him was devouring his sandwich with gusto. "It's got pickles!" he exclaimed.

"I remember pickles!" a girl down the table said happily.

Dalaya didn't seem interested in her own plate of corndogs, and Kenth eyed them as she concentrated on her artwork. He ought to be hungry, but he wasn't. He was just tired. Maybe he'd rest when Dalaya went down for her nap. "Daddy likes fish," she said very seriously.

"Who doesn't like fish?" Toren agreed, returning to the table with a plate for himself and Carina. "Want to hit the buffet before it gets picked over? I don't think that Mrs. James is going to put out more."

"I have a sandwich," Kenth said, gesturing at Dalaya's drawing. "Thanks, though."

"There," Dalaya said with satisfaction, putting down the crayon.

A sandwich materialized on the table between them as the drawing burst into flame and dissolved into purple ash.

It was the ugliest sandwich that Kenth had ever seen, with limp slices of bread and bold green fern leaves falling out of it. As he stared at it, it jerked and wiggled, and he cautiously lifted the bread to find a gasping goldfish twitching on the soggy bread.

The children seemed interested in the sudden appearance of a magical real-fish sandwich, but not very surprised. Carina and Toren both stared, and the housekeeper who had been handing out linen napkins and refilling water glasses dropped her pitcher with a clang.

This did excite the children, and it precipitated a scramble for towels to clean up the water and corral the scattered ice cubes.

"We need water for the fish!" Carina cried in alarm and she captured it and started to dump it into a glass.

"No, that's ice water, you'll kill it!" Toren warned while she was still cupping the spasming fish. "We need room temperature water! And it should sit for a while to let the pH stabilize!"

"How do you know so much about goldfish!?" Carina wanted to know.

"I had aspirations of being a marine biologist at one point," Toren said merrily.

"All this time, I thought you wanted to be a sled dog," she teased him back.

"That was Tray!" Toren protested.

The kids laughed and clapped their hands as staff scurried to find something to put the fish in and clean up the mess.

"Did I do it wrong?" Dalaya asked plaintively, slipping her hand into Kenth's.

Kenth stared down at her. "No, of course not, it was wonderful, darling. We were just surprised, that's all."

A cup of appropriately warm water was hastily brought and the fish was slipped into it and then watched anxiously by everyone present as it slowly circled. It didn't seem to show any indication of immediately turning belly up.

Kenth felt Mackenzie's arrival before he saw her, that swirl of anticipation and interest that wasn't all his in his chest.

Raval came in from the opposite entrance. "Why do I have to be here?" he demanded. "I was in the middle of a project."

"When are you not in the middle of a project?" Fask asked wryly.

Of *course*, Fask had taken control of the situation as soon as it had been reported to him. Kenth caught himself scowling and looked around at Mackenzie because her distress was chattering at his heart. He could feel how flustered she felt, how attracted she was, how she tried to dampen all of her feelings…and mostly failed.

"Mrs. James said you needed me," she said quietly.

The story was told, with excited additions from the audience of all ages.

Mackenzie shook her head. "I can't tell you anything about a spell that is already cast, but I don't think that I have ever heard of a drawing working as the base of magic. It is always words, with focused intention. You must be a remarkable talent, Dalaya."

Dalaya had been sulking and wilting at the negative attention, dismayed because her present had been met with such a distinct lack of appreciation. She brightened at Mackenzie's words. "I'm a marker telant!" she agreed. She didn't offer to get out of Kenth's lap.

Raval was no more help than Mackenzie and considerably less good-natured about it. "Why would I know anything?" he demanded. He stayed a distance from the milling kids, looking at them warily. "I've never summoned a goldfish."

The goldfish was finally tracked down to Nathan, the man in charge of the kennels, who had a fish tank in his rooms and gravely confirmed that one was missing.

"Transportation of an object is a much simpler intention than creation," Mackenzie explained. "I presume that Dalaya's focus was on ingredients that she thought Kenth would like, but stripped down to its most basic parts. When you're first learning to write or draw, you use gross simplifications—a half-circle for a smile, stick figures. They aren't things you'd do in fine art or even spoken sentences, but she managed to concentrate her power into these concepts with her artwork."

She was nervous, with everyone listening respectfully to her, and Kenth wished he could reassure her that she was doing great without undermining her hard-won autonomy. He was also wondering if he should have eaten something earlier, because he felt light-headed and tired.

"As hard as anyone tries to define something specifically, there are always going to be gaps. You can describe an object perfectly, but miss some vital statistic, like its size, or its skin, and magic will fill in those gaps. This is something that I've heard people call chaos magic, and it's very, very dangerous. If you cast a spell with too many uncertainties, you can't predict what will happen, and usually, they don't work at all."

She seemed to find some strength in Kenth's gaze. "I could spell a fire and it might be a little spark or a wild fire that takes out an entire city block; the results would be completely random. A caster has to specify where the fire should be, how long it lasts, how it is dispelled, where it goes, what it burns, where it gets its fuel. Dalaya wanted a sandwich. It would appear that she thought of bread, of greens, of fish, and drew those things. The magic filled in the many missing parts and summoned what was nearest."

"Daddy likes fish," Dalaya said, voice muffled in Kenth's shirt.

Toren laughed, shaking his head. "Remind me not to ask her for moose."

CHAPTER 12

Mackenzie was used to Amara coming to her for answers about magic, but it had always been fraught, trying to explain what seemed so obvious to her. She was never sure when Amara would accept her words or fly into a temper over something not working the way she wanted it to. She didn't know when Amara would believe her explanations or call her qualifications into question. She was no caster herself. Magic didn't even work on her. What could she possibly know about it?

When she explained chaos magic, Amara sometimes accused her of simply getting it wrong, or being incapable of reading the spell the way she said she could.

But here, they seemed to take her at face value. She was Kenth's mate before she was anything else.

Fask clearly didn't trust her, but Mackenzie wasn't sure if that was because she'd been a Hand of the Cause or because she was Kenth's mate and Fask bore his brother obvious ill will.

The gathered royals chewed over the information that she gave them and looked at Raval for confirmation.

Raval shrugged. "That matches everything I know," he agreed. "Me and my eyebrows learned pretty quickly that you have to be really, really specific if you don't want some wild outcomes, and spells simply won't work if you don't have enough details down."

"How do we keep eyebrow—and goldfish—endangering incidents to a minimum?" Fask wanted to know, frowning at her. "We should take away her drawing supplies."

Kenth's arms tightened around Dalaya as she made a sound of protest.

"Do you like to draw?" Mackenzie asked her.

Dalaya nodded enthusiastically.

"But it's not always to make real sandwiches, right?" Mackenzie persisted. "Sometimes it's just to draw? You don't have to think about the drawing *making* things, you can just draw."

Dalaya's nod was less excited.

"Probably we should do that for a while," Mackenzie said coaxingly.

"I'll want you to monitor her at all times," Fask said to Kenth, frowning. "Make sure that there are no accidents."

"I'm sure she didn't mean any harm," Kenth said firmly.

"Tell that to the goldfish," Fask muttered.

Kenth glared at him but didn't respond. Mackenzie was honestly surprised at his restraint and cast a concerned glance at him. Ever since their return, he'd become more and more subdued, and she couldn't help but wonder if she'd done something wrong. He hadn't pressed her about being his mate or made a single move in her direction, and she didn't think that it was just that he was being courteous.

He seemed...exhausted.

That morning, at the breakfast table, he'd been quiet, but he looked more drawn now, pale and almost gaunt. She thought that maybe it was the haircut, which had once again drastically changed his appearance, but when she dared to look at him carefully, she thought there was an unhealthy cast to his skin.

They were all tired, of course, and he must have been so worried about his daughter. Maybe it was all just catching up with him.

Mackenzie could certainly relate. It had only been two days since she left everything she'd ever known and thrown her lot in with the enemy, met a prince who claimed she was his mate, rescued a dozen children, and returned to a palace in Alaska where she was given a suite of rooms, a wardrobe of clothing, and a buffet of rich food.

Mrs. James herded the other children back out to the hall, which had been transformed into a gigantic playroom. Mackenzie went to help her, feeling more than a little responsible for the fact that the palace was being overrun by kids.

"Daddy?"

There was a crash behind her and Mackenzie turned back to find that Kenth had fallen backward out of his chair and was getting up slowly, holding his shoulder.

"Kenth?" Toren asked.

Tray was standing in alarm. "What's wrong?"

"What are you doing, Kenth?" That was Fask, sounding suspicious, as if he thought that Kenth was playacting.

Kenth growled wordlessly in reply, clutching at his shoulder like he was trying to claw something out of it. "Got shot," he said between his teeth.

"And you didn't tell us?" Tray sounded like he was trying to joke but knew it wasn't funny.

"Doesn't hurt," Kenth said curtly.

"It sure looks like it hurts now," Toren said, as if he was desperate for levity.

"Doesn't hurt *me*," Kenth growled. "It's my dragon."

"Daddy?!" Dalaya said again, the pitch of her voice rising as Kenth tried to take a step and fell to his knees instead, twisting in pain. She was clinging to the chair he'd fallen out of and looked like she wasn't sure what to do.

"Get the kids out of here," Fask said crisply. He scanned the rapt crowd. "Toren, Tray, open up his shirt, let's look at the wound. Which shoulder?"

First Mrs. James and then Carina tried to get Dalaya's hand to pull her back, but the little girl scanned the crowd and spotted Mackenzie, making a beeline through the princes and their mates to get to her and throw panicked arms around her.

Mackenzie scooped her up and held her close, staring through the crowd at Kenth.

He struggled as Toren and Tray held him down, snapping like a rabid dog as they stripped off his shirt and exposed his skin.

Mackenzie hung back, watching helplessly, and was glad that Dalaya seemed to want to hide her face in Mackenzie's hair rather than try to see what was going on. Toren whistled and Carina turned her head away in horror, but she couldn't see what they'd exposed.

Fask looked up and met her eyes through the others. "What is this? What happened to him?"

Mackenzie clutched at Dalaya harder as the others parted to let her through.

Mrs. James appeared at her side to take the little girl and Mackenzie reluctantly handed her over, murmuring reassurances that she didn't exactly believe. Dalaya wept and screamed and struggled, and Mackenzie had to peel her off like a cat trying to evade a carrier. The door closing behind Mrs. James muffled her cries.

Mackenzie went hesitantly to Kenth's side and knelt.

They had uncovered an angry red wound in Kenth's shoulder. No one needed to wonder if it was magic—the gash was writhing with black tendrils of smoke. Kenth's whole body arched in pain and he was gritting his teeth so tightly that Mackenzie could hear them grinding.

"Well?"

Mackenzie met Fask's gaze and wondered at the concern that she saw there. As fraught as his relationship was with his brother, he really did care that Kenth was suffering. Is that what family was? Loving someone even when you were utterly at odds?

"I can't see spells once they've been cast," she said quietly, wishing she had any other answer to give him. She wanted to be helpful, to prove that they hadn't been wrong to take her in, and instead, she was more useless than ever. She wracked her head for any spell she'd ever read that could do this. "Amara had a tiny blade that was poisonous to dragons. Perhaps she modified it so that it could be fired from a gun? I...don't know." *Don't be hysterical, don't panic, stay steady.*

"Glad," Kenth gritted out.

Mackenzie wished she dared to touch him, maybe even take his hand—they were both balled into fists. But she was keenly aware of everyone watching them, and she was afraid she would do more harm than good. "Glad?" she repeated.

"Glad you can't feel this," he gasped.

Mackenzie's heart squeezed. He was thinking about her right now? Going through this, he was grateful that he could spare her his own suffering? Mackenzie felt tears well up in her eyes and willed them back with all her might. "Hang on," she whispered. "Fight it. All spells fade."

"Da-da—where is Dalaya?" He reached up and clawed at Mackenzie, taking hold of her shirt.

"Dalaya is with Mrs. James," Mackenzie told him, boldly taking his hand into hers and cupping it. "She's safe, she's okay."

"Take care of her," he begged through clenched teeth. "Protect her."

"I will," Mackenzie promised, completely unable to keep her tears in now. "I will."

He made a noise mostly composed of G's and spit, then his head hit the floor behind him so hard that Mackenzie feared he'd crack his skull. Two of his brothers leaned in to hold him still, but it was unnecessary because after he arched up with a cry of pain, he went completely limp.

For a terrible moment, Mackenzie thought he was dead and the depth of her despair shocked her. She barely knew this man, this prince of Alaska. They had met only a few days before and she couldn't feel the bond that he swore they had. She owed him a great debt, and at some point, she must have attached more of her heart to him than she ever meant to or realized that she had, because the idea of him dying was like pitching off a cliff into darkness.

She could no longer imagine her world without him.

"He's still breathing," Rian said hoarsely and Mackenzie drew in a jagged breath of her own. She still had Kenth's hand in hers and she clutched it like a lifeline.

"Well," Fask said roughly. "Let's get him into a bed and give him a fighting chance to get through this and outlast the spell."

Mackenzie might have thought he was being cavalier if she had not seen the concern and worry in his face, he sounded so chilly. She let go of Kenth's hand to back up out of the way.

The jokes and mock complaining that they did through meals and meetings was strangely missing as Tray and Toren each took a side and they hauled him limply upright, then got an arm under each knee to carry him out of the dining room. From the outside, it only looked like maybe Kenth had overindulged, his head lolling to one side.

But there was a grim air to the room that was not so easily shaken. Mackenzie dragged the palm of her hand across her tear-wet cheek and knew that she must look frightening. She had to keep herself under control, because Dalaya, who was still wailing her protest from the next room, needed her to be strong.

Mackenzie had promised to protect her, and that's all she could do now.

CHAPTER 13

Kenth's dragon was screaming.

Ever since he was a small child, his dragon had been the *steady* part of his soul: older, wiser, and always under control, even when Kenth himself felt ready to fly into a temper. Sometimes he wondered what his life would have been like without being constantly reined in by the superior and smug supernatural creature who shared his head.

But whatever had happened to him, whatever had struck him so innocuously during their escape, it had wormed its way into him and found his dragon.

It was deeply alarming to have him writhing and out of control now, shrieking in agony. His dragon was supposed to be untouchable, bigger and stronger than Kenth, and it shook the very foundation of his worldview to be the one trying to keep them calm.

We'll get through this, he insisted. *You can outlast this.*

What had Mackenzie said?

All spells fade.

All his dragon could do was scream.

It was like having a fever, he was burning inside, too much heat and pain to contain inside his human body.

If he shifted?

Could he shift?

Kenth tried, but his dragon was incapable of focusing his magic and changing their form. There was only pain. Only black fire. He was consumed from within.

His anchor was Mackenzie, with her worry and future love like a bright light that was the only thing keeping him from collapsing into ash. She was afraid for him now, she adored and trusted him then, she was everywhere and nowhere, the flutter of her mind like a cooling touch, but when Kenth tried to reach for her, she slid somewhere else.

All he could do was chase her through his own thoughts and listen to his dragon howl.

CHAPTER 14

Dalaya and Mackenzie sized each other up.

Dalaya sat on her bed, perched on a pink bedspread with her arms crossed. Mackenzie sat across from her on a couch.

What was she supposed to do with the child? Dalaya was much younger than any children Mackenzie had cared for before. Amara found infants annoying and didn't want toddlers underfoot. She frequently brought up how much trouble having young Mackenzie around had been, and how generous Amara was to have kept her at all.

There were still tears glittering on Dalaya's cheeks, and her mouth was set in a defiant frown that suggested there were more where they had come from. At least she had stopped sobbing, finally sitting up after Mrs. James left in defeat.

"Are you hungry?" Mackenzie offered.

Dalaya shook her head.

"Do you...need to go potty?" Was a kid of this age potty-trained? Characterization of children in books seemed wildly variable, from unconvincingly capable infants to helpless school children.

Dalaya shook her head again, more vigorously, so that her wavy dark hair bobbed around her face.

Mackenzie eyed the television. She knew the theory behind it, but she had no idea how to actually operate it.

"Do you want to play?"

The room was full of toys. The purpose of some of them was obvious, like the stuffed animals scattered across the bed, and the dolls leaning by an elaborate dollhouse. Some of them, Mackenzie couldn't identify. Many of the things were still in bright packaging. A tiny kitchen was set up underneath the window, with small scale pots and pans and fake food.

Dalaya raked her gaze around the room and shook her head.

"There are some games in the next room," Mackenzie offered. There was a pile of them on the table in the sitting room between Dalaya's bedroom and Kenth's, still wrapped in plastic. She had been disappointed that Monopoly was not one of the choices; she had read about the game but not ever been able to figure out how it would work. She guessed that these were games for younger people, but she wasn't familiar with any of them. She'd been glad to have a full deck of cards as a child.

This seemed to be of reluctant interest to Dalaya, so Mackenzie went out to get them. The door to Kenth's bedroom was open and several of the brothers were gathered there, having a quiet, urgent conversation. She tried not to stare as she gathered up the boxes, or eavesdrop too obviously. As she turned back, she nearly tripped over Dalaya, who had silently followed her.

"Is Daddy going to be okay?" she asked plaintively.

Mackenzie knelt so that she could offer Dalaya a hug

with her free arm. "He'll be fine," she said, wishing she was as certain as she sounded. "If this kind of magic doesn't kill you all at once, it can usually be shaken off when the spell fades."

As soon as she'd said it, Mackenzie wondered if it was too frank. Should children be protected from the idea of death altogether? She certainly never was. Death was always an acceptable price in the struggle for the Cause.

"Let's go play a game," she suggested firmly, and she drew the door shut behind them.

Dalaya was more interested in opening all of the games and looking at all the tiny little pieces and markers and cards than she was in actually playing them, and she collected her favorite parts from each one. Mackenzie went along with that, and moved them from the table to an empty shelf when Dalaya wanted to play restaurant.

"I've never eaten at a restaurant," she told Dalaya as she tied the little apron around the girl's waist.

"I have to make a menu!" Dalaya said officiously.

A quick search turned up no crayons or pens or blank paper. Mackenzie suspected that Fask played some role in that; he probably didn't want to risk more goldfish sandwiches. They used the rules from one of the games, and Dalaya told her what to order, then gathered it all from the little kitchen and "cooked" it vigorously.

Mackenzie pretended to relish her meal and Dalaya had her order another. And another. And *another*.

"I'm so full!" she protested, holding her stomach. The game had gotten painfully tedious, but Dalaya seemed distracted from worrying about her father, so Mackenzie went along with it until a minor inconvenience—the plastic apple was green instead of red—had the girl threatening tears again.

"Would you like to go for a little walk?" Mackenzie

suggested. "We could find the real kitchen and get a snack."

Dalaya liked this idea, but she hesitated at the door out to the hall. "Does Daddy need a stuffed animal?"

When Mackenzie hesitated, Dalaya ran back to her bed and picked out a floppy, fluffy lion. They went together to his bedroom, where Toren was sitting beside Kenth's bed doing something on his phone.

Dalaya shyly stepped forward with her offering, Mackenzie hovering even more shyly behind.

"He'll love that!" Toren said, too cheerfully for the grim room. He tucked the lion in beside Kenth, who stirred and moaned.

Dalaya put her hand into Mackenzie's and clung tight to her side as they left.

At first, they just wandered the halls, stopping briefly to check in on the older kids, who were getting haircuts and new clothes. A pair of guards trailed them discretely.

Dalaya quickly dragged her on and she kept up a lively conversation with very little of Mackenzie's help. "Daddy likes fish, do you like fish?"

"I suppose so."

"I like some fish, I like salmon, but I don't like tuna fish," Dalaya offered. "I like corn dogs and pizza and I don't like onions and I like Little Tree Friends and I want to be an astronaut and I like that flower cup!"

"Let's not touch it," Mackenzie said. "It looks fragile!"

They found the kitchen and were fed so many warm cookies that Dalaya later had trouble eating her dinner in the informal dining hall with the other children. She grew more cranky and tearful as the meal went on, and they left her plate half full to retire back to her rooms for bed. Was Mackenzie supposed to have put her down for a nap in the afternoon? She felt helplessly out of her league chasing Dalaya, and wondered if she looked as lost as she felt.

Dalaya was exhausted but completely unwilling to go to bed and had a dozen things she insisted that she needed to do first: Take a bath. Go potty. Get a drink of water. Go potty again. Brush her teeth. Another drink of water.

Mackenzie tucked her in with a dozen stuffed animals, read her a story, and finally curled up on the bed next to her until Dalaya's eyes grew heavy at last and she fell into a deep, boneless sleep.

Mackenzie wasn't much less exhausted, but she didn't think she could sleep, so after a moment, she screwed up her courage and left Dalaya's bedroom to cross the dark sitting room.

CHAPTER 15

Raval was sitting next to Kenth, scowling at a book that he didn't appear to actually be reading. "What do you want?" he said when he finally looked up and saw her.

Mackenzie thought he didn't actually mean it quite as coldly as it sounded. He had that intensely focused kind of personality that rubbed some people wrong, she thought.

"I'd like to sit with him for a while," Mackenzie said shyly.

It was a bold request, and it assumed a level of trust that she probably hadn't earned.

But Raval nodded. "Sure. If you need anything, just holler. The door's open and someone will hear." He actually looked relieved, like Mackenzie had saved him some trouble.

Maybe she had.

She took the seat that he abandoned and curled her feet up into it underneath her. It was cool in the room, but Kenth was sweating. Occasionally, he groaned and writhed, but he never woke. The blankets had come down off his shoulders and the magic wound undulated with evil, black strands. The stuffed lion had been tossed to the far side of the bed.

Mackenzie wondered if he'd die.

The idea made that empty place inside her echo in agony. He'd been so kind to her, so understanding of all the things that were wrong with her, so patient with all of her hesitation. He'd brightened her existence, shown her affection that Mackenzie had never imagined. He'd trusted her with his daughter, with his whole heart.

If she wasn't broken to magic, could she use the mate spell to somehow save him? Would her strength be able to anchor him through that connection? That was certainly what happened in the books she'd read. True love always had the power to save.

Maybe if she loved him hard enough?

But all that Mackenzie knew about love she had learned from fiction. She wasn't even sure if she loved him at all, or if she only thought that she should. He was the best thing that had ever happened to her and he was certainly strong and handsome, but was what she felt for him only attraction and her own starved and confused heart? Did she only feel these things for him because he was so sure that she *would* love him? When did prophecy become self-fulfilling?

Mackenzie cast her gaze to Kenth's pale, sweaty face and wondered if it would assume too much to take his limp hand in hers.

She giggled when she actually caught herself looking around for a tub of cool water and a sponge that she could wipe his brow with. She had clearly read entirely too much of the *wrong* kind of fiction.

She did take up his hand after a moment, but it was so cool and unresponsive, so completely unlike the other times that she'd held it, even when he was sleeping, that she put it back down almost at once.

Then she picked it right up again, determined to give him any comfort that she could. People in comas could hear people talking to them, couldn't they?

"Kenth," she started.

Her voice in the quiet room was too weird.

"Kenth, please hang on." Her voice cracked and it was a moment before she could go on with confidence that she wasn't going to break down crying.

What did you say to someone who was dying? Beg him to fight? Apologize for dragging him into this mess in the first place? Confess her feelings? She couldn't untangle the emotions in her heart, let alone on her tongue.

But she could thank him and make sure that he knew how grateful she was.

"Thank you," she said softly, making circles on his limp hand with her thumb as if she could rub life back into him. "Thank you for trusting me. For getting the kids away from Amara. For standing up for me. For making me welcome in your home. Thank you for all of your kindness and goodness and for looking at me like you see some worth in me. Thank you for seeing me at all."

Should I kiss him? she suddenly wondered, and as soon as she thought of it, she had to try, casting a quick look at the open door. It was awkward—his bed was huge, and he wasn't right at the edge, so she had to lean over quite far, and his lips were dry and cool and unresponsive.

The sinuous black magic at his shoulder continued to pulse and sizzle.

This wasn't a fairy tale. Or it wasn't true love. Or maybe her heart wasn't strong enough.

Mackenzie settled back into the chair and fought back

tears. After a few moments, she spoke again. "It was worth a try," she said.

The silence was too much again after a while, so Mackenzie tried speaking again. "Fask says he's going to hire a tutor for the kids. It might take a while to find their families. They don't remember much that's helpful—I think that the trance stone has an effect on memories and I'm kind of glad for that. They're really grateful to be here, but they don't have to think about how awful it was."

Mackenzie spent the night at his side, sometimes talking, sometimes dozing in the big chair. She woke up every time that he moaned or stirred, and every time that someone walked past the open door of the sitting room.

By morning, her eyes were gritty, and her voice was hoarse. Rian came in to spell her, and Mackenzie had time for a swift shower before Dalaya woke up.

Dalaya was clingier than she'd been the day before and more prone to bursting into tears for any reason, but Mackenzie reminded herself to be patient and was rewarded with dozens of fragile hugs and little feather kisses. Dalaya showed her how to work the television and they were both briefly enthralled over a children's show with puppets and bright colors.

Commercials were the weirdest things. It was a feed from the United States, with loud advertisements for bizarre toys and baby supplies. Mackenzie evaluated them in terms of propaganda, and judged them very effective indeed; she caught herself craving tiny biscuits and dollhouses.

She didn't want to rely too much on screen-time, as addictive as she'd heard it could be, so she and Dalaya explored the house and grounds. After they played hide-and-seek with the older kids for a while, Tray invited them out to meet his puppies.

CHAPTER 15

"It's the best therapy," he said knowingly to Mackenzie.

Mackenzie could not imagine a better distraction. The puppies were at the size that was all paw and ears. They were plush and cuddly, as interested in being snuggled as they were in chasing balls and wrestling with each other. Dalaya squealed in delight and waded into their play fearlessly.

They spent an hour there, romping in the straw until both Mackenzie and Dalaya were covered in fur and dog spit and Dalaya was getting clumsy with exhaustion. Even the puppies were wearing out.

The little girl took a brief nap that she swore she didn't need while Mackenzie lay down on the couch in her room.

She woke to find Dalaya gazing thoughtfully down at her and immediately felt guilty for falling asleep. "Whoops!" she said, dragging herself upright. Dalaya crawled up onto the couch next to her and snuggled into her side.

"Is Daddy going to be okay?" she asked plaintively.

Mackenzie had been doing her best to keep Dalaya fully occupied at all times, and she'd been glad to stay busy herself. Every time there was a lull, she thought about the pain in his face and the despair of losing him.

Should she lie and say that Kenth was going to be fine even though she feared he wouldn't be? Should she be honest and say that it didn't look good?

"Your Daddy is really strong," Mackenzie finally said, squeezing Dalaya close. "It's just a spell, and all spells fade. All he has to do is hang on a little longer."

"What happens to me?"

Mackenzie heard the *if* at the end of the sentence. *What happens to me if Kenth dies?* had been a sentence in her head since his collapse.

"Your uncles will take care of you," Mackenzie promised. "They all love you very much."

Dalaya's arms tightened around her. She was strong for her tiny size. "I don't want you to go away," she said into Mackenzie's armpit.

"I don't want to go away, either," Mackenzie said. "But your Daddy is going to be fine." Did it sound convincing? "All spells fade." It was her mantra, to keep herself hoping that it was true.

That night, it took nearly two hours of gentle argument to get Dalaya to stay in bed. She had to go potty. The stuffed animals were in the wrong places. The curtains were scary. The room was too big. Her pillow was upside down. She was hungry.

Mackenzie indulged her, for the most part. They split a package of cheese crackers sitting on the floor so that crumbs wouldn't get in the bed—Mackenzie wasn't sure how she managed it, but Dalaya was a master at getting crumbs and sticky fingerprints everywhere. She tied the curtains back, even though that made the windows into dark mirrors that were more frightening than curtains in Mackenzie's opinion. She waited patiently at the bathroom door, listening to Dalaya play with the toilet paper roll.

Finally, Dalaya lay down in her bed and slept, with Mackenzie on the floor holding her hand.

Mackenzie slipped from her grip and crept across the sitting room to Kenth's open door.

The Majorcan dragon, Drayger, was sitting in what Mackenzie considered her chair, flipping through a magazine. It looked like Leinani was on the cover, beautiful, unsmiling, and dressed in island formalwear. The title of the cover article was *Which Royal Brother?*

He looked up at her entrance and gave her a crooked grin. "You want this seat?" he offered.

Mackenzie nodded shyly and he stood up and offered it to her with a bow and a flourish. "My lady," he said formally. Then, more seriously, "How are you holding up?"

Mackenzie was touched by the question. Everyone asked about Dalaya a lot, but not so much about her.

"I'm good," she said vaguely. Then she added honestly, "It's a lot."

Drayger laughed kindly. "You haven't exactly had an easy time of it," he said sympathetically. "I...get it. I mean, we have a lot in common."

Mackenzie was too tired to pretend to understand; she could only stare at him rather stupidly. What did she have in common with a bastard prince?

"I get how it feels to realize that you've been on the wrong side of things and you want to make up for it," he explained. "You did know that I was hired to kill Toren and Carina?"

Mackenzie blinked at him. "I did *not* know that." Should she be afraid of him?

"I wasn't *going* to," Drayger said swiftly. "But that kind of offer makes you take a hard look at your life and wonder how you got so desperate that it looked like you might."

"Desperate people do a lot of desperate things," Mackenzie agreed, surprised by her sympathy for him. "Who hired you?"

"I was kind of hoping you could tell me," Drayger said. "I don't know and I've wondered a few times if it was related to your Cause."

"It's not *my* Cause," Mackenzie said sharply. She gentled her voice. "Amara didn't involve me in that part of her business. I'm sorry, I can't confirm that for you."

"Fair enough," Drayger said. He glanced down at Kenth. "It must be nice to have a little proof."

"Proof?" Mackenzie was back to feeling stupid.

"That you aren't just the sum of your past. The Compact wouldn't have picked you for Kenth's mate if you weren't a good person." Drayger actually sounded wistful and then looked embarrassed. "Anyway, enjoy your time," he said with forced merriment. "He's a dead bore of a conversationalist, all moans and muttering, so I hope you brought something to read."

He edged out past Mackenzie. "Good luck," he said over his shoulder as he left.

Mackenzie wasn't sure if he was talking to her, or to Kenth, or if he meant it as a joke.

This time, she gathered up Kenth's hand with more determination and told him in detail how Dalaya's day had been, lingering over the happy moments. She stuffed back all of her fears and her longing to simply lie down at the edge of the bed and weep. She might not be able to feel Kenth through their mate bond, but maybe she could give *him* hope.

And if he had hope, maybe he could hang on long enough to outlast the spell.

CHAPTER 16

It had always been an asset to have his dragon's strength and spirit, and Kenth often wondered if his dragon felt as if Kenth was an undesirable dead weight, a fragile human shell compared to his dragon magnificence.

But his dragon had fallen.

It felt like Kenth was on fire from the inside out, and he knew that if it wasn't for his own dogged stubbornness, they would have given up days ago and let death find them peace. All he had to do was outlast the enchantment, but it was like trying to keep his feet in a roaring river full of spring ice, buffeted in every direction by stinging hornets.

He had never known pain at this level and he could feel his will to keep fighting gradually wane, dragged down by his dragon's unending screams of pain as he burned in a fiery pit of magic. It would be easier just to drift away and let the river of agony sweep him to the sea.

"It's not *that* bad. Stop feeling sorry for yourself."

This unfamiliar voice brooked no nonsense, and Kenth was shaken from his reverie of self-pity and pain to find that there was someone else in his head where only his dragon had ever been.

He had the impression of an old woman, silver-haired and dressed in dark robes of black feathers covered in stars.

"I'm not done with you yet," she said sharply. "The others still need you and I am going to be very cross if you disturb my plan by giving up now, this close to the end."

"What plan? How long?" Kenth begged. "How long will it be like this?" If he had a finish line to put his sights on, maybe it would be bearable.

She shook her head, and her hair was like dandelion fluff, with seeds floating off of her to layer over Kenth like soft snow. "All spells fade," she said sadly. "I can't help you, you can only help yourself now."

"How long?" Kenth sobbed. "How much longer?"

"Time isn't the important factor here," she said firmly. "Love is. Hold on for that."

Then she was gone, and he was alone with his dragon's pain.

Somehow, though, the dandelion fluff she'd left behind seemed to make the screams a little less loud, like cotton absorbing echoes. Kenth thought fixedly of Dalaya and Mackenzie, vowing to persevere as long as it took.

All spells faded.

All he had to do was hang on.

CHAPTER 17

The third night, it was Fask who was sitting by Kenth's bed when Dalaya was finally in bed.

Mackenzie almost turned back at the door to his bedroom, but instead raised her chin when Fask looked up from the papers he was studying and caught sight of her.

They stayed that way for some measure of time, Mackenzie not quite brave enough to come into the room, Fask not asking her to leave or enter.

It seemed like a long while, but she thought it was probably only a few moments before Fask closed his folder and stood up, gesturing to the chair that he vacated.

Should she apologize for being trouble? Mackenzie wondered as she drifted into the room. Should she offer more help? She was too tired and heartsick to think of anything. "How is he?"

"He looks worse," Fask said.

He sounded cold, but Mackenzie wondered how much of it was a mask.

Kenth was his brother. However at odds they were with

each other, there was blood between them, and she was sure that Fask did not want his brother to die.

Fask cleared his throat and edged out past her without further discussion, leaving Mackenzie alone with Kenth.

Kenth did look worse, the pulsating black smog completely engulfing his shoulder now. He didn't make any noises and he was distressingly still. Mackenzie had disliked his uncomfortable, restless stirring, but now she wished he would do it again, because this was much more unsettling.

Mackenzie pulled the blanket to block the sight of the terrible magic and put her hand over his as she sat beside him.

"Dalaya has been so good," she said, because Kenth would want to know that most of all. "She has all the older kids wrapped around her fingers. They all want to play with her and pretend to babysit. She's being terrifically spoiled, all your brothers are giving her presents and wardrobes of clothes and toys. Mrs. James is the worst of them, making corn dogs and pizza every night and even for breakfast because that's what Dalaya likes."

She spoke on, nonsense about life in the castle, the weather, playing with Tray's beloved dogs. "He tried to give me a puppy, can you believe it? Said it's an Alaskan bride tradition. He joked that maybe Fask would've kept Leinani if he'd tried giving her a puppy. Fask didn't laugh, but everyone else did."

She told him about Fask's latest plan for counteracting Amara's subversive media campaign, which mostly comprised of trying to drown them out with good press. She cataloged their progress—not much—towards finding the families of Amara's caster children. Eventually, she lapsed into silence, out of words and hope.

"Menzie?"

Mackenzie had started to doze in the warm room. It

was her third night of almost no sleep and she jerked upright again at the sound of Dalaya's voice from the open door.

"Aren't you supposed to be in bed?" Mackenzie scolded gently.

"I slept," Dalaya said. "I couldn't anymore."

Mackenzie stood and found that one of her feet was asleep. She limped to Dalaya and picked her up, not sure if she should let the little girl see how weak and still Kenth was. "Are you worried about your Daddy?" she asked. Was that baby talk? Should she not do that? She would have to ask Tania if there were any books about raising children in the library.

Not that she would need them if Kenth died. There was no way that anyone was going to let a cultist—however reformed—take custody of a princess, just by virtue of a dusty old piece of magic contract. The idea of losing Dalaya gave Mackenzie a stab of grief. She'd become very fond of the child in their time together.

Dalaya wrapped her arms around Mackenzie's neck and leaned a warm, plump cheek against her. "Uh-huh."

Mackenzie tightened her embrace, hoping it was of some comfort. Certainly, holding onto her was some comfort to Mackenzie.

"You want to sit with me for a while?" she suggested.

They watched Kenth's struggle to breathe in silence for a while, Dalaya so still in her arms that Mackenzie thought she might go back to sleep.

"Do you have a Mommy?" Dalaya asked, suddenly enough that Mackenzie actually startled.

"I...ah..." Mackenzie wasn't sure how to answer the question. There was a mother that she had no memories of, wrapped in all of Amara's lies and falsehoods, but Amara had sometimes called herself Mackenzie's mother.

Did she count Amara's hot-and-cold affection? Sometimes the woman insisted that Mackenzie give her kisses and embraces, and other times didn't speak to her for days. And before that... "I did once," she decided was a truthful answer, if non-specific.

"I did, too," Dalaya said thoughtfully. "She makes Daddy sad."

Mackenzie tightened her arms around Dalaya. No one ever spoke of who Dalaya's mother was, and she wasn't sure how much of it was genuinely unknown, as Dalaya herself had been, and how much was the kind of dirty laundry that simply wasn't spoken of. Certainly, Fask had more information than the rest of the family, and Mackenzie wondered how Dalaya's mother was tied up in the animosity between the brothers. Had Kenth been married? Was Dalaya illegitimate?

Mackenzie realized that she had almost no working knowledge of the actual royal structure. She knew Amara's poisonous stories of their power and greed, and she knew the fanciful tales of her favorite books.

The actual truth seemed to lie somewhere between the two kinds of fiction. She was surprised by how *human* the royal family was, appreciating the irony of the description applied to actual *dragon shifters*. For all of their wealth and polish and privilege, they were earthy and good-hearted. They had opened their home to almost a dozen lost children without a word of complaint.

They laughed and loved and talked about their body functions and teased each other. She watched them lift each other up and thought that they were, if nothing else, as complicated as anyone else.

Dalaya squirmed, and Mackenzie put her down. There was a pad of paper and a pen on the table beside the bed and Dalaya began playing with them. Mackenzie watched her write her name in blocky irregularly capitalized letters.

"What are you writing, Dalaya?"

"I'm fixing Daddy," she said confidently.

"Wait..." Mackenzie told her in alarm as she felt the magic intentions start to form.

Dalaya was only five, with a five-year-old's hazy understanding of the world and a poor grasp of cause and effect. Mackenzie didn't have the magic-shaping orb that Amara used to focus her young casters, and she knew that the core of chaos magic without the structure of a spell might be disastrous. Most magic that didn't follow the strict rules simply failed to work, but Dalaya's seemed to work whether she had a structure for it to hang on or not.

If Dalaya started thinking about food or fantasy, would her spell have some unexpected result? Would she accidentally manifest a puppy from the kennels or animate a favorite toy?

His daughter could kill Kenth as easily as she could cure him.

Mackenzie closed her eyes and looked at it with the hollow place inside of her.

Most spells had a skeleton of *must*s and *shall*s, forming an immediate purpose and a distinct outcome that Mackenzie could effortlessly predict, even when they were sloppy and had holes of logic and possibility.

Dalaya's spell was impossibly squishy. It had her purpose woven all throughout it, to *fix-Daddy*, with an underscore of *want-to-have-fun* and a dangerous thread of *fear-safe-protect*, with curious tones of *keep-bind-mine*. Every time that Mackenzie touched it, testing some outcome, it changed, like the shimmer over a soap bubble. It looked like there were a dozen different ways to activate it and no way to halt it.

Unpredictable, Mackenzie thought. It was more chaos than magic, and she didn't trust that it would do anything that either of them intended it to. Dalaya didn't understand enough about what was wrong with Kenth to fix it and it was too dangerous to try.

She opened her eyes to figure out how to tell Dalaya gently that they shouldn't use it when Kenth arched up the bed with a cry of pain, flailing wildly and knocking over a bedside light with a resounding crash. The black smoke was swirling faster now, and it looked like it was going to consume him entirely.

Dalaya gave a whimper of fear and backed into Mackenzie. Not sure how much she could or should protect her from seeing what surely had to be Kenth's last moment, Mackenzie reached down and gathered the sobbing girl up into her arms.

There were footsteps, drawn by the commotion and the broken lamp.

"What happened?" Mrs. James wanted to know, leading a housekeeper and Nathan, the man from the kennels. "Kenth? Is this…?"

"I don't know," Mackenzie said, her chest squeezing. *Don't panic, don't panic, don't be afraid, bury what you're feeling, be empty inside…* The last thing Kenth needed right now was her complicating matters by having a panic attack through their mate bond while he was fighting for his life.

Dalaya was trembling in her arms. "We have to help him," the little girl said, her voice thin and wavery.

Mackenzie realized she had crumpled the spell in her hand, probably smearing the ink. She opened her fingers and dropped it.

"We have to get back, Dalaya," she said, turning away with her. It was too terrible to let her watch, surely.

But Dalaya stiffened and resisted. Mackenzie didn't

want to struggle with the girl too obviously in front of the others and was surprised by how strong she was.

"Dalaya, Dalaya! No!"

The girl wriggled from her grasp, snatching the wadded spell up from the floor and dodging Mrs. James and the kennel-keeper in order to fling herself up onto the bed.

The spell landed square on Kenth's still chest, bounced, and rolled off.

Mackenzie thought it had failed to activate, then watched in horror as it burst into a moment of flame before disintegrating in the blink of an eye. She felt the weird hollow suck of magic as if she was standing in a momentary stream of fast-moving water.

The oozing black smoke that was now covering most of Kenth sucked down into a tiny cloud and shot to Dalaya, vanishing into her.

"What was that?" Fask roared from the doorway.

Dalaya was crying in earnest now, as Mrs. James dragged her back from Kenth. Then Dalaya gave a gasp and went limp in Mrs. James' arms as Kenth drew a deep, rasping breath and sat bolt upright. There was a weird, voiceless wail, and he collapsed back down onto the bed with his eyes closed.

There was no sign of the black magic.

"What is happening?" Fask demanded.

Mackenzie braved his anger to go to where Dalaya was being lifted by Mrs. James from the bed, her head lolling back as she sobbed piteously and kicked her legs and pushed away.

"Is she hurt?" Mrs. James asked tenderly, gathering her up despite the girl's objections to cradle her close. "Oh, is she hurt?" She looked desperately at Mackenzie, who was staring past her to Kenth.

He was breathing easily now, his chest rising and falling evenly.

Nathan leaned down and took his pulse. "His heart's steady and strong," he said.

Kenth was alive. He was going to be okay. Why was she going to cry *now?*

"What happened?" Fask had stalked around the bed to catch her by one arm. "What did you *do?*"

"I don't know," Mackenzie confessed with a sob. "She drew a spell, but it was all chaos, no structure, I wasn't going to let her activate it, but he started to seize, and… and…" He was going to live, she reminded herself. "Dalaya didn't really understand how a body works or how to fix Kenth, so I think she just…took the poison magic into herself. Because she's not a dragon, it had nothing to do, and it…ended at last."

Mrs. James sucked in her breath. "If she had been a dragon…?"

"This is completely careless and reckless!" Fask shouted. "Why did you let her do this?" His hand was hard around her arm and he looked furious.

"I couldn't stop her!" Mackenzie protested. "I'm sorry, I tried to!"

Dalaya had stopped fighting against Mrs. James and was weeping limply on the bed.

Fask let go of Mackenzie to go to Dalaya, but she drew away from his touch and cried for Mackenzie.

Mackenzie opened her arms and Dalaya ran to her, clambering up to cling like an octopus, all her limbs wrapping tight around her. "I need to breathe," Mackenzie reminded her, repositioning her arm carefully.

"You were told not to let her do magic," Fask growled, as if Dalaya wasn't right there listening. "You understood the danger of it. Clearly, we cannot trust your word."

CHAPTER 17

"I didn't tell her to do it! I would have stopped her," Mackenzie said as bravely as she could manage. It actually helped to have Dalaya in her arms. She might not have stood up for herself, but having something smaller and more helpless to protect helped her face the disapproval of the oldest prince. It had been the same with Amara; she would never have defied the leader if she had not had other people to think of.

Fask's glare made her shiver and hold Dalaya tighter. She wasn't sure if Fask disliked her for daring to be Kenth's mate, for being Amara's hand, or for some other reason, but his distrust for her had definitely crystallized into an active antipathy.

"You shouldn't have let her get that far," Fask scolded her loudly. "It was reckless, and it proves that your judgment is flawed. I want Dalaya removed from your care immediately."

Dalaya gave a cry of protest and clung even harder to Mackenzie.

"Whatever she did, it worked," Mrs. James interjected firmly. "He's breathing evenly, and his heart rate's steady. Look at his shoulder."

Mackenzie's own heart was racing, and she wondered if she dared to argue on her own behalf. Kenth had trusted Dalaya to *her*. She didn't want to defy Fask, but she was even less willing to betray Kenth's last conscious charge.

"What's going on?" Carina was standing in the doorway, wrapped in a bathrobe.

Beside her, Toren was wearing nothing but a pair of boxers. "Is Kenth okay?" he asked anxiously.

Behind them, Tray and Leinani came crowding. "What happened?" the prince demanded. "Did Kenth...?"

"Kenth is finally sleeping restfully!" Mrs. James said sharply. "And you lot can get out, all of you, because you are not helping him any. Not you!" she said to Mackenzie. "You and the girl can stay. I want to check her over. I want to see that the magic hasn't harmed her, and his highness will want to see you *both* when he wakes."

She faced down Fask with a steely glare. *"You* may go," she said in a voice that brooked no argument.

One of the other princes gave a muffled bark of laughter.

Fask, his face like a thunderstorm, looked like he was going to argue, then he shot Mackenzie a warning look and stormed out, herding his brothers and their mates before him.

Mrs. James gave Mackenzie an apologetic look. "He's more worried for Kenth than he'd like to admit," she said, then she picked up the pen and the pad of paper that was still lying on the bedside table and followed him.

"Did I do the wrong thing?" Dalaya asked plaintively. "Was I bad?"

Mackenzie plopped down in the chair beside Kenth's bed before her knees gave out and she lost her grip on the little girl because she was heavier than she looked and Mackenzie felt weak with relief. Dropping a princess was probably not a good way to stay in royal graces.

"You weren't bad," she said to Dalaya, as reassuringly as she could. "You were a hero. You did a brave thing and it worked. You saved him. *You saved him.*"

Only Dalaya herself, sniffling into her collarbone, kept Mackenzie from bursting into hysterical tears of her own on the spot. Kenth was going to be okay.

She hadn't realized the depths of her affection for this man she barely knew. Maybe she didn't have a working mate bond, but in the few exciting days since they'd met, they had been through enough that she knew his measure. He was a good man, a complicated, passionate prince, with a gentle heart and a fierce front. He loved his daughter, his family, and his country...even Fask, Mackenzie thought, in his own angry way.

And most amazing of all, he loved Mackenzie, or he would, and Mackenzie was shaken by how desperately she needed that.

Amara had spoken often of love, of devotion, but never actually gave it. Kenth didn't say it, but it was obvious in everything he did, in the way that he treated Dalaya, in every interaction with his brothers, in his respect, in all his casual gestures, and in how he looked at Mackenzie.

No one had ever looked at her that way.

Not just with desire, but with adoration. He saw something in her that he *valued*. Not as a tool, for her curious magical gift, not for her body, though Mackenzie thought he might appreciate that, too, but for her whole self.

Mackenzie didn't have the advantage of a mate bond to tell her how perfect they might be together, or share what he was feeling, but he was unselfconsciously transparent with his emotions and she knew that she was not immune to the intoxicating possibility of being genuinely loved.

It certainly didn't hurt that he was the most handsome man she'd ever met, or that he was built like a model and moved like a dancer. He was the fulfillment of every dream she'd ever had.

She realized that Dalaya had gone limp in her arms, her tears turned to exhausted sleep. She didn't even stir when Mrs. James came back, checked her vitals, and declared her fit.

"His highness will be asleep now for a few hours at least, I think," Mrs. James said quietly. "You should go put her to bed and get some sleep yourself, if you can. I'll make sure someone calls you when he wakes."

Mackenzie gave her an obedient nod and gathered Dalaya bonelessly up.

The little girl gave a sigh and stirred as she was tucked into bed, then fell back to sleep at once. Mackenzie left a tender kiss on her forehead before she crept away to the couch for a few restless hours of sleep.

CHAPTER 18

Unconsciousness had been such a relief after the pain-sliced haze of the poison battling his dragon that Kenth almost didn't want to wake up.

Finally, he opened gritty eyes and wondered how long he'd been asleep.

"Kenth? Oh, you're awake, what a relief. I'll go get them..." Mrs. James bustled out before Kenth could stop her or pretend quickly enough to go back to sleep so that maybe he could. He moved his limbs hesitantly, and his dragon seemed to stretch in his head like a cat.

It has been a long while, his dragon observed. All of Kenth's muscles had a curious stiffness, as if they'd forgotten how to move properly.

Are you all right again? he asked his dragon.

I am undamaged, his dragon insisted, and Kenth had a sense of his usual smugness. *If nothing else, I am even stronger for the struggle.*

The darkness behind the drawn curtains didn't tell Kenth what time of day it was; winter in Alaska's interior was dark well into the morning, with only a few hours of daylight before the sun set again early in the afternoon. He blearily wondered who Mrs. James was fetching and whether he wanted to see them. Fask was probably going to be on his case about something.

But it wasn't Fask that came barreling in with Mrs. James. It was Dalaya, with Mackenzie at her heels.

"My two favorite girls," Kenth said as Dalaya jumped for the bed and Mrs. James cautioned her to be careful.

He only thought that it might be disrespectful to call Mackenzie a girl after the hoarse words left his mouth and he struggled to sit up. Females didn't seem like a great improvement, but Mackenzie didn't feel offended, anyway. She was deeply relieved for him, warm and yearning in what felt like a promising new way. The worst of her prickly doubts seemed to have been scrubbed away. With worry? It was hard to pick out what was future and what was past from what was now. She certainly felt *happy* to see him, and that was good enough for Kenth.

Dalaya was flinging eager arms around him. "I missed you, Daddy!" she mumbled into his shoulder and Kenth hugged her close and gave her affectionate tickles until she shrieked with delight.

"I missed you, too," he said when she had rolled away giggling across his broad bed.

"Are you all better now?" she wanted to know, sitting up seriously. "Menzie said I made you better."

"Did you give me a kiss while I slept?" Kenth teased her.

"No," Dalaya said with a frown. "I drew a picture."

Kenth shot Mackenzie a startled look and found affirmation in her face and in her crisp nod. "She thought she could help and drew a spell before I could stop her. Apparently, it worked. You look quite…recovered."

Kenth felt her wash of desire a scant moment before

she blushed and he realized that he was not wearing anything other than a pair of boxers, his chest bared by blankets when he sat up.

"I helped," Dalaya said with satisfaction. Then she added frankly, "You're smelly."

"I could use a shower," Kenth agreed. "Can you go with Mrs. James so I can talk with Miss Mackenzie for a few minutes first?"

Mrs. James, sniffling suspiciously, nodded. "I'll have someone come in later and make everything up with fresh bedding."

"I took a bath last night," Dalaya said, crawling to the edge of the bed and carefully slipping down onto the floor. "I like the squeezy-fish." She gladly took Mrs. James's hand. "Can I have fish crackers and watch TV?"

Kenth made a face. "She wasn't kidding. I *am* smelly. How long was I out?"

Mackenzie sat gingerly down in the chair next to the bed. It was a chair that hadn't been there when he last remembered thinking clearly, and he wondered if Mackenzie had spent much time there.

"Three nights," Mackenzie said. "Everyone thought you were going to die."

Although her voice was steady, Kenth could feel the surge of emotion and fear and confusion that welled up in her. "*I* thought you were going to die."

She didn't have to explain her thoughts, and when Kenth offered her his hand, she took it without hesitation. Lacing his fingers into his calmed the worst of her turmoil and Kenth let his thumb make comforting circles on the back of her hand but offered nothing else. "I'm apparently fine," he said as lightly as he could. "Just needed the right Get Well card."

Then, because he knew it concerned her, he promised,

"You wouldn't have been thrown out, even if I'd shuffled past this mortal coil."

Her chagrin was hot and guilty. "It's not that...I wasn't..."

"I know," he said swiftly. "You were genuinely worried for me. I *know*. I just want to make sure that *you* know that you're safe here, no matter what. You have selflessly helped us against Amara. And you were tapped by the Compact and not even Fask would dare to defy that old scrap of dragonhide. I will protect you with my life, but I am not the only one in your corner now." He could not quite resist drawing her hand up to his mouth and laying a careful kiss on it. His lips were cracked and dry. "Also, my brothers know that if they were ever unkind to you, I'd come back and haunt them forever."

Her mouth crooked into a tearful smile, and Kenth could feel the concern shed from her. "Thank you," she said softly. She took her hand back slowly.

"No problem," Kenth said gravely. He could tell that his bare chest was still distracting Mackenzie and tried to decide if it would disturb her more if he stood up to find a shirt in just his sleeping shorts. He was also finding that other needs were waking, most urgent among them a need to visit the bathroom. "I've always wanted to be able to walk through walls and throw things around without touching them. In fact, I'm beginning to regret that you yanked me back from that certain death. I would love to drive Fask crazy. I'd screw up his filing system so hard."

"Everyone says that Tray is the prankster of your brothers," Mackenzie said with a smile. "I see that they were mistaken."

"Tray is an amateur," Kenth scoffed. "He lacks imagination. Also, he's always been easy to pin things on." He winked at Mackenzie and she laughed.

They sobered together. "What did Dalaya do?" he had to ask. "Catch me up?"

Mackenzie pursed her lips. "I'm not really sure," she admitted. "I've never seen anything like it. The kids that Amara had were all old enough to write, and that's the only way I'd ever seen spells work before Dalaya. But she has this *level of intention* that is really advanced for her age, and she seems to be able to hold that same level of concentration that writing spells requires. Amara needed a device to get her kids to focus at that level, and they were even older."

She hitched her breath in. "It was a terrible risk," she confessed. "I wouldn't have let her make the spell at all. And when she did, I wasn't actually going to let her cast it, it was so much chaos, almost no structure, I couldn't predict it, but then you were…and she just…" She was blind panic and bone-deep exhaustion in his head.

"Hey, hey," Kenth said gently. He risked disturbing her sensibilities to push back the blanket and swing his legs off the bed. "It worked out, didn't it?" He was still holding her hand and used it to pull her to sit on the bed next to him. "I'm okay now, thanks to you."

She slowly let herself sag into him and cry softly. "I thought you were going to die," she confessed, and she didn't have to explain how that made her feel. Kenth was getting a head full of her fear and relief and worry.

"I didn't," Kenth told her, stroking her hair as she cried out the worst of her tension. "I'm all better now, my dragon is back to being an obnoxious and opinionated fixture in my head. Everything is going to be just fine."

Hey! his dragon said, both amused and offended.

You just spent three days straight screaming in my head, Kenth reminded him. *A little payback is due.*

After a moment, Mackenzie extracted herself carefully

from his embrace and she sat shyly beside him. Kenth thought she might be trying not to stare at his legs.

A terrible thought occurred to him. "Could Amara have *done* something to Dalaya?" he asked.

"Something to activate her latent talent?" Mackenzie considered that with him. "She didn't have her for very long, and if she had something that would do that, I didn't know about it. But it's the *kind* of thing that Amara would do. There were spells she wouldn't show me, that she always kept locked away."

Then, because Kenth knew that they must both thinking about it, he guessed, "Do you think Amara tried to do that to *you?*"

Mackenzie's mouth went thin. "It would certainly be true to character for her to try to make me into a magical tool. Though clearly she failed with me, and not with Dalaya."

Kenth regretted saying the hypothesis out loud. Did she think of herself as a failure? If he were smooth like one of his brothers, or just better at people, he thought he'd know what to say to convince her that she wasn't. Tray would probably have a joke at hand, something light-hearted to make her laugh.

He loved it when she laughed.

But he couldn't think of anything funny, so he settled for enjoying how she tried not to look at him as he slid off of the bed and tested his legs.

"I, oh, do you need some…help?" she squeaked. "I could call one of your brothers. They gave me a phone…"

"I think they'll work," Kenth decided, flexing his knees. "I can get to the bathroom myself."

Mackenzie, her fluster as obvious on her face and in her fluttering hands as it was in her head, looked away and gave a start.

Fask was in the doorway. "Mrs. James said you'd woken." He exchanged a look with Mackenzie that Kenth couldn't quite put words to. "If you will excuse us?"

"Of course." Kenth hated how Mackenzie shrank under Fask's appraisal. "I'll...see you later," she said timidly to Kenth. Then she hastily rose and beat a swift retreat, edging carefully around Fask as he came into the room.

"You didn't have to chase her out," Kenth growled at Fask.

"Peace," Fask said, and if he didn't say it peacefully, he did spread his hands in a gesture of truce. "How are you feeling?"

Kenth bit back his initial response to brush Fask off altogether. "I've been better," he said honestly. "I kind of feel like I've been trampled by a herd of musk ox and then struck by lightning. And I really need to piss."

He only swore because he knew it would offend Fask's delicate sensibilities, so he was surprised when his brother laughed.

"It's good to have you back, Kenth," he said gruffly. "I mean, back in the world of the living, and...back home. I'm especially glad that Dalaya isn't a secret anymore."

Kenth was surprised. They'd done nothing but fight since his return and he was sure that Fask resented his presence. "Thank you for keeping that secret," he said. "I know you didn't agree with it."

"It's the stupidest thing you've done yet," Fask said shortly. "And that's saying a lot."

That was the brother Kenth remembered. "Well, I'll endeavor to do something even more stupid, so we can put that behind us."

They glared at each other and then laughed, and Kenth thought for a moment that they might embrace.

Instead, Fask cleared his throat and sobered. "I'm sorry to bother you so soon, but...there are complications."

"Dalaya?" Kenth said swiftly.

"Not Dalaya. The rest of Small Kingdoms. I've been talking with the other kings and...we're not the only ones being hit. There have been attempts on the Compact at seven other kingdoms that I know of, and...some of them were successful. There are pages missing."

"What would that mean?" Kenth asked in concern.

"I don't know," Fask said. "But I don't think it's good."

"Mackenzie might be able to tell us," Kenth pointed out. "She could read the Compact and see what it does, like she did with Leinani's ring. She could tell if something was wrong with it."

He expected Fask to argue about trusting Mackenzie too much again, to suggest that the mate bond was false, but Fask only frowned. "She's proved useful," he said. Then, grudgingly, "And you should know that she spent every night here with you. She cared for Dalaya and the children all day and sat with you all night."

Kenth's heart gave a little twang.

"But..."

There was always a *but* with Fask.

"Spit it out, brother," Kenth said crossly. "I still have to piss."

"She let Dalaya do magic on you," Fask reminded him. "She *says* she tried to stop her, but no one was here to witness that."

"You try keeping a five-year-old from doing something they insist on," Kenth said with a chuckle. "It saved my life, by anyway, and it's hard to be mad about that."

"Did she tell you how it worked?" Fask asked.

"Dalaya drew a spell that cured me."

"Your daughter took the magic into herself," Fask said.

CHAPTER 18

Kenth hissed in his breath.

"If she'd been a dragon, it would have killed her," Fask pointed out. "You barely survived it yourself, with a full-grown dragon. If she had her dragon, the spell would have consumed it and taken the human host right along with it."

"But she's *not* a dragon," Kenth said sharply, to hide how the idea had disturbed him. "The spell couldn't hurt her."

"She's the age where she could be, at any time now," Fask said firmly. "It was a reckless chance." He looked down at his hands. "I'm glad, in retrospect, that it happened like it did, because I'm pretty sure we would have lost you otherwise, but it was a reckless and stupid choice. You should think long and hard about Mackenzie's role in it and how she might have been willing to risk your daughter to keep her golden ticket."

Kenth laughed. If Fask was trying to make him doubt Mackenzie, he was barking up entirely the wrong tree.

"You're wrong about her," he said fiercely. "Mackenzie is smart and talented. She's got a great big heart and soul of absolute steel. She isn't reckless, though I grant that she might have been desperate. Fask, she's my other half. I trust her. I trust her with my life, and I trust her with my daughter. Don't overlook the asset that she could be to us in our fight."

"Is this *our* fight?" Fask asked pointedly. "You aren't going to just take your daughter and run away again?"

"Amara made it personal," Kenth snapped. "I'm not going anywhere until she's taken care of and I know that my daughter will be safe. And Mackenzie can *help* us with that."

Fask's look was complicated, with resignation and reservation, and possibly even grudging respect. "I hope you're right," he said. "And we could use every advantage we have right now. Let's show her the Compact. But I'm coming with you when you go."

"Chaperone us if you want to," Kenth said with a shrug, "but unless you plan to come to the bathroom with me right now, I suggest that you leave now and ask Mrs. James to make me a pile of hamburgers to regain my strength. I'm going empty my bladder and take a long shower, because I smell like a musk ox."

"A musk ox who rolled in a skunk cabbage," Fask said frankly. "Come and find us in the informal dining room when you feel up to it; we're going over the latest reports from our intelligence and Captain Luke has some concerns."

"I'll be there," Kenth agreed.

CHAPTER 19

The whole feeling in the castle had changed drastically and Mackenzie didn't think that it was only because she'd had her first night of solid sleep since Kenth's collapse.

For days, the prospect of Kenth dying had darkened everyone's mood, and the rescued children were distraught and uncomfortable, creeping around like kicked puppies. The news outside of the castle was dismal—Mackenzie wasn't privy to the war meetings and wasn't sure what the news actually was, but she heard whispered mentions of assassination attempts and the theft of magical items. Leinani's mother and father had left to help protect Mo'orea following some civil unrest, and even Drayger seemed to be taking the recent developments seriously.

Drayger, by all accounts, never took anything seriously.

But Kenth's dramatic recovery had altered the mood considerably. The children, finally starting to believe that they were free and shaking off the last strains of Amara's spells, brightened and began to play in earnest, encouraged by all of the castle staff and the royalty themselves. They raced each other down the long hallways and the wings echoed with laughter.

And Kenth was going to live.

Mackenzie thought he was going to kiss her no less than four times that morning and once after lunch.

Each time, they were interrupted before a quiet exchange and a simple touch could turn into something more—twice by Dalaya, who was oblivious to the moment of anticipation she was barreling into, once by Mrs. James, who winked at them, and once by Fask, who walked in on them as Kenth seemed on the brink of taking her into his arms.

Those big, gorgeous arms that Mackenzie could not keep herself from thinking about.

She told himself that she was probably reading too much into a lingering glance and an expression of gratitude, but it didn't change the fact that she was dying for Kenth to take those liberties. He had to know what she wanted, didn't he? Did he not want it himself?

She wondered if she imagined that the daylight itself felt longer. She knew that the days were lengthening again, but she didn't think it should be a change so radical in the first few days of January that she would be able to notice it.

But it really did seem like the sun was higher than it had been even just the day before, and that it cast more light through the tops of the snow-covered spruce trees.

She took a decadent shower after lunch and went to find Kenth in the afternoon, only to discover that he was deep in a discussion with Fask and Rian. He looked up when she wandered through the castle to find him in the informal dining room and flashed her a quick smile, but didn't invite her in to join the serious discussion.

She smiled back and wondered what she should do next. The older kids were being fitted for clothing. Should she offer to help with that? She wasn't sorry to have a little space to herself after three days of Dalaya's incessant chatter and her clinging, but she also missed having an obvious duty…and she missed Dalaya's sunny and distracting presence.

Mackenzie was definitely not the only one in the castle who had successfully been wrapped around Dalaya's finger; Tray and Toren had stolen her after lunch to go play with the puppies.

"Mackenzie? We're all meeting in the library for a bit of an unwind with wine before dinner, would you like to join us?" Carina was standing in the hallway behind Mackenzie and her smile was welcoming.

Mackenzie glanced around. Kenth was clearly embroiled in a heated discussion with Fask. She didn't need a mate bond to know that he was angry. He broke off from his tirade to glance her way, and Mackenzie felt guilty for distracting him with her insecurity. She needed to find her own way and make her own decisions. She didn't need him to tell her that it was okay to meet with other people and maybe even make friends.

She'd loved romance books with heroes and adventures, but books about friends had always been her favorites. Would she do it right? Would they like her? Making friends seemed more fraught than manners at dinner or being interrogated.

Mackenzie smiled at Carina. "I'd like that," she said bravely.

Carina looked genuinely happy with her answer. "It seems like we've been kind of non-stop since you got here," she said, falling cheerfully into step with Mackenzie. "I mean, a daring rescue, followed by a whole lot of kids, and Kenth's poisoning and…we haven't really had a chance to just hang out."

Hanging out was a thing that normal people did, Mackenzie reminded herself. It was what normal people with normal childhoods were used to.

She hoped that Kenth's argument with Fask wasn't interrupted by the sudden unease that was coursing through Mackenzie. Communicating with a five-year-old was one thing, but Dalaya wasn't old enough to understand how deeply unsocialized Mackenzie really was.

The others all had a background steeped in media and culture that she'd never known, had watched television and movies that Mackenzie hadn't even heard of. She was going to look so stupid and out of place. She steeled herself.

The library was enormous, with tall arching ceilings, huge windows, and a dozen comfortable reading nooks. There were heavy curtains pulled over the windows, and it was all rich and cozy. Mackenzie resisted her impulse to lean down and see if the carpet was as plush as it looked with her fingers.

There was a wet bar in one corner of the room, and Mackenzie was equal parts appalled by the mixture of purpose and delighted by the touch. Why shouldn't a library have a bar?

"Would you like a glass of wine?" Leinani asked, her voice low and serene. Of all of them, Mackenzie found the Mo'orean dragon princess the most intimidating. She had the most polished manners, everything about her perfectly composed and under control.

Leinani had also seen Mackenzie working for the Cause, helping Amara, and while Mackenzie thought that helping them escape counted for something, she still struggled with her guilt over what had happened to Leinani and Tray.

A drink tempted Mackenzie, but she didn't have a lot

of experience with alcohol and suspected that it would go straight to her head. She had read enough to guess what a disaster that might be.

She definitely did not want to throw up on princess shoes.

"I shouldn't," she said reluctantly. Would they think she was rude?

"I'm not drinking, either," Tania said kindly as she took a seat in a recliner chair with a hook for her cane. "It interferes with my medication."

No one had been specific about what kind of condition Tania had, but she walked with a limp and carried a cane. Rian sometimes showed up alone to meals and said that she was indisposed, often taking a plate away with him. Everyone always accepted that news with complete understanding, and Mackenzie felt like she shouldn't pry.

"Would you like some fruit juice or a soda instead?" Leinani suggested kindly.

A drink to hold onto might be helpful. Sipping it would give her something to do when the conversation ran away without her, as it surely would. "Soda, please."

Leinani investigated the choices in the little fridge under the bar. "Root beer or cola?"

Mackenzie accepted a cola and only later wondered if she would regret the caffeine; she was still running precious low on sleep. Tania asked for a root beer. Leinani brought out the drinks with the gracious flourish of someone who regularly poured formal teas, dined with royalty, and entertained ambassadors. The drinks were in tall glasses with perfectly formed ice cubes.

They all found comfortable seats near Tania and spoke of the weather, briefly, exclaiming over the cold and dark. Leinani even managed to *complain* elegantly. The others made a concentrated effort to include Mackenzie, and she admitted that she had seen snow before, but never in such abundance.

"It isn't as cold as I expected," she added shyly.

Tania asked if she had read much about Alaska, and to Mackenzie's surprise, they had enjoyed several of the same classical books that gave them rich common ground for conversation, leaving Carina and Leinani out for a short time.

Finally, at a lag in the discourse, Carina asked what she had clearly been longing to ask for some time. "You really don't feel the mate bond at all? *Nothing?*"

Did they doubt the bond, like Fask clearly did, or suspect that it was a trick?

Mackenzie reached inside herself, wishing with all of her heart that any part of her own longing and interest in Kenth might not be her own, or even not her own *now*. She could not deny that she felt connected to him, but it was a connection that their time and adventure together had forged, and all of the feelings that she had for him were based on his kindness to her, on his heroic actions, and on his gorgeous physique and face. She could not blame any of what *she* felt on magic.

She spread her hands helplessly and shook her head. Even without alcohol in her drink, she felt bold enough to counter with her own question. "What is it like, for you?"

"Was," Tania corrected. "It's nothing now, of course. All spells fade."

"Not that I feel *nothing* now," Leinani was quick to add. "Because I still have...very warm emotions for Tray. But the mate bond itself is gone."

"What *was* it like, then?" Mackenzie was determined not to sit aside afraid through every conversation and lose her chance at making friends. Besides, she was dying to know more about the mate bond from the women who had actually gone through it.

Carina laughed. "I thought I was going a little crazy. This cute park ranger shows up and I'm feeling all the stuff *he's* feeling and all this crazy stuff that I *will* feel, plus I'm absolutely sure that I'm about to be arrested, and holy moly, horny as a goat, and I don't even know how to sort it all out. It's like having someone shout constantly in your ear. But kind of nice, you know. It doesn't really leave you wondering if you'll suit each other, because you just *know* that you will. Because you feel who he is inside."

Tania smiled. "For me, it was a little like listening to a song that you know will make you cry, and you tell yourself you won't cry this time, but you totally do. The feelings are there, but they aren't…they aren't your real *now* feelings. You're kind of a step off from them. Sort of? It's hard to explain. It's a little dreamlike."

"I thought it was *nice*, though," Carina said.

Tania made a noise of agreement and nodded. "I always felt safe with Rian. Protected. He never felt like a stranger, even though it was still all thrilling and new. Like the best of all worlds, we were comfortable together but still got all the new love exhilaration."

Leinani tipped her head thoughtfully to the side and wrinkled her brow. Mackenzie wondered if she practiced the gesture, it was so charming. "I do think my dragon augmented the feelings," she said. "Dragons are sensitive to magic, you know, and sometimes it was overwhelming how much we felt of each other, how raw and intense it was."

"It was sometimes a lot," Tania agreed.

"But I knew that I could trust Tray," Leinani continued. "That part didn't feel like magic, it felt like…nothing else was possible, like it was a fundamental truth of the world, that Tray was a good person and that we would love each other." She laughed and for a moment, the polite mask slipped from her face to betray a wash of complicated emotion. "Even when we were trying really hard not to."

Mackenzie sipped her cold soda and the ice rattled against her teeth. "I wish I could feel that," she said wistfully.

"Kenth certainly does," Carina said firmly, as if she had just realized that Mackenzie must be doubting her own bond. "It's so obvious that you were made for each other. I mean, maybe you don't have his feelings and your future rattling around in your head, but he's definitely picking up on yours. And it's clear to anyone with eyes that the guy totally *adores* you."

Leinani smirked a little and nodded her agreement. "Head over heels," she said.

Tania chuckled.

Carina leaned forward in her chair. "Are the two of you…?"

Mackenzie blushed. "No! I mean, leaving aside that he's been in a coma for three days…"

They all laughed and agreed that his recovery was a great relief to everyone.

Just as Mackenzie thought that the conversation had moved safely aside from the topic of sex, Carina grinned at her and said, "It's okay, you know. It's not like a regency novel where women have to maintain their virginity or whatever."

"The regency period wasn't actually that puritanical," Tania said gravely. "People confuse it with the Victorian era a lot…" Then, unexpectedly, she winked at Mackenzie. "And the modern era certainly doesn't care."

"Oh, the tabloids *care*," Leinani said drolly. "But what

have they ever gotten right? They'll just make up what they don't know anyway. You should see what they wrote about Tray and me while we were away." She rolled her eyes in a very un-princessly way.

Mackenzie laughed along with the others, but a little sheepishly. She wished she had a better handle on modern culture. They weren't really implying that she should be sleeping with Kenth...*were they?*

"Are you a virgin?" Carina asked bluntly.

"You can't just ask her that," Tania said in outrage.

"Sorry, I'm dying to know!" Carina said, and her laughter felt kind. "You don't have to tell me," she told Mackenzie. "I'm just a cloddish peasant, don't mind me."

Mackenzie sucked her breath in. "I'm...not a virgin," she confessed. "But I've definitely read a *lot* more than I've experienced." She exchanged a sideways look with Tania, who gave her a sly, knowing smile. Several of the books they had discussed had not been prudish.

"Don't wait," Leinani added unexpectedly. "You don't know what could happen."

They were all quiet for a moment, all of them probably thinking of Kenth's collapse, and the three days that they thought he would die.

"You've been so great with Dalaya," Tania said kindly. "With all the kids, really."

"And you were so brave during the rescue," Carina added. She was lounging sideways in her chair, her shoes kicked off to show striped stockings. "I can only imagine how terrifying it must have been!"

"I wasn't that much help," Mackenzie tried to demure. "There were dragons..."

Leinani herself gave a little scoff. "Don't sell yourself short. You were exceptionally courageous. We would not have been successful without you."

Mackenzie opened her mouth and closed it again, pleased and delighted by their praise, but not entirely sure what to do with it. Was she supposed to say thank you?

The moment passed before she could decide, but it didn't feel awkward when the discussion moved on.

The conversation was like a dance. Sometimes, Mackenzie and Tania were aligned with their mutual love of books against the other two as they talked about their favorite television shows and movies. Tania watched almost no popular media, and if it was by choice rather than strict cult edict on her part, it still gave them a place of common ground.

"I've watched Little Tree Friends three times," Mackenzie added, and she was delighted when everyone thought that was funny, as she'd intended it to be.

She and Leinani, on the other hand, had both experienced Amara's control. When Carina was dismissive of her threat and wished that they could get out and explore the little city of Fairbanks, Leinani was quick to side with Mackenzie, who cautioned that it was easy to underestimate the power that Amara had or her clever patience.

"She's dangerous and unhinged, and Mackenzie knows that best of all of us," Leinani said gravely, and Mackenzie had a dizzy moment of feeling included that was topped by a quick, warm handclasp from the princess.

Carina, she gradually realized, had all the same feelings of being outclassed that Mackenzie herself did. She was quick with her self-deprecating jokes about being the grubby American commoner in the group, but there was a wry truth beneath her words that Mackenzie recognized.

Tania had a polished and educated confidence, and Leinani could not have hidden her royal manners if she had even bothered trying, but Carina and Mackenzie were both floundering through the unspoken expectations of a class they hadn't been born to or educated into. They shared several sideways looks, and Carina rolled her eyes and snorted whenever things got too snooty.

Mackenzie's glass was refilled again with soda, and Carina slouched into her chair even more after a second glass of wine. Even Leinani looked like she was listing comfortably, just a little. The two of them were talking about television again, and Tania was browsing one of the bookshelves.

Mackenzie wondered what alcohol would have been like, whether it could possibly top this amazing feeling of being included, of being seen and listened to, by people she was already cautiously fond of. Mackenzie wasn't sure how much weight to give Dalaya's affection, and the Compact constrained Kenth to see her favorably. But she thought these women might actually *like* her, and be her *friends* even if circumstances were different.

"Oh, they're expecting us at dinner!" Leinani exclaimed suddenly. "We've let the time slip by." She began to gather up their glasses, but Carina stopped her.

"Wait, first a toast," she insisted. "I've got a little left."

The others all lifted their glasses to her and paused, Mackenzie following along with what everyone else was doing. She'd read about toasts, but had never been part of one.

"To the queens of Alaska," Carina said. "We are all amazing."

She was a part of something, Mackenzie thought in wonder, draining the last of her soda-flavored ice melt from the bottom of her glass as the others did the same. Something she *wanted* to be a part of.

Nothing in her life had ever tasted so sweet.

CHAPTER 20

Kenth always knew where Mackenzie was, with a hazy certainty, not a sense of what she was doing exactly, but a general underlying yearning that had a direction to it. If he wasn't careful, he would wander that way, and he more than once found himself starting down the hallway towards her room instead of the other direction to the kitchen or up to the dining room.

He managed to keep himself from lurking in front of her bedroom like some kind of stalker, but sometimes it was hard to make himself turn away from the lodestone pull of her.

So, he happened to be walking down the long back hall rather than the front hall towards the dining hall when the library door opened and the princesses spilled out.

Two princesses, anyway—Leinani and Carina were both official royalty, but Tania wouldn't be a princess until she married Rian, and Mackenzie would only be a princess if she married Kenth.

For a moment, Kenth thought it was the idea of marrying her that had set him unexpectedly on fire, then realized that it wasn't his own feelings at all. Mackenzie had caught sight of him, and her spike of desire was absolutely *unmistakable.*

She was usually good at keeping herself on an even keel, her emotions carefully reined in—sometimes Kenth felt furious to think how she must have been raised, to have such practice denying her own true nature. She was careful not to enjoy anything too much, like she was afraid to lose it.

This wasn't the first time she had wanted him; Kenth knew very well that she was attracted to him, and her thoughts about him—when she allowed herself to think of him at all—had an underlying warmth of affection that was gradually growing.

It was hard to separate what was 'could be' from what she felt now, but Kenth knew she was fond of him, and he was longing to share with her all the feelings that she was *going* to have.

Carina was giggling and Kenth realized that he had stopped in the middle of the hallway and was simply staring at Mackenzie.

"Hello, Kenth," the crown princess said brightly. "We were just heading to our rooms to freshen up before dinner. Perhaps you'd like to escort Mackenzie to *her* room?"

Kenth could feel Mackenzie's nervousness, and he scowled at Carina with a warning shake of his head. At least there seemed to be an undercurrent of amusement to Mackenzie's chagrin.

"You're not helping," Leinani scolded Carina, but her eyes sparkled and she smirked knowingly at Kenth.

"Sorry, I haven't had loads of princess training like you." Was Carina tipsy?

"C'mon, you two," Tania said, herding them down the

hall before her with her cane like they were wayward goats. "Leave them in peace."

"Sorry," Mackenzie said to her feet when they had gone. "They invited me for drinks in the library."

"You don't need to apologize," Kenth growled, only hearing how harsh he sounded after he spoke. She didn't have the advantage of knowing in her own head that he was all butterflies and yearning inside, that he wanted only her happiness, forever. She could only see the prince, argumentative and abrasive, the black sheep of the family. The screw-up. The grouch.

And somehow, still, she wanted him.

They were alone in the hallway now. If he moved just one step further towards her, he could bend down and kiss her, could take her into his arms and show her what he was feeling, how crazy she was making him. But wanting him wasn't the same as inviting him, and if he took advantage of his position and his power over her, he could never forgive himself.

"I can tell how hard this is for you," he said as gently as he could. "I know that you...doubt. You doubt me, and you doubt yourself."

Mackenzie gave him a grateful look that was amplified by a wave of warm feeling.

"You've been very kind," she said awkwardly. "And it looks like you're feeling a lot better."

Kenth wasn't sure why that made her desire so much more intense, but it was hard to keep his own response to her under control. "I am, thank you." He made a show of smelling an armpit. "I showered, too. I promise I'm much better company now than I have been the past few days!"

He wasn't sure what was more rewarding, the way her eyes crinkled into laughter, or the wave of amusement that came off of her at his joking. For the first time in his life, he thought he understood why Tray was such a ham.

"I'm...glad," she said with a chuckle. "Fask was really mad."

"Did he yell at you?" Kenth knew his brother brought out the worst in him every time, but the idea of him being mean to Mackenzie made him feel like his mouth was full of nails.

He moved closer to her, without meaning to, and she had to look up at him, her eyes big and dark.

The memory of Fask gave her a ripple of fear and shame and guilt. Did she disbelieve that she had done the right thing? Everyone else had been sure that he would not have survived without it. Kenth set his teeth. "If he made you feel bad..."

"He thought that it was reckless," Mackenzie said meekly. "I *had* promised to keep Dalaya from trying more magic..."

"Fask is a..." Kenth swallowed the descriptor he wanted to use. "A tool," he settled on. "He's too tied up in rules and what's proper and safe. He won't take necessary risks. He's too busy trying to be important to have a heart."

"He has a heart," Mackenzie protested. "Fask clearly cares about protecting his country *and* his family."

"As long as the family falls in line," Kenth growled. Then, "Argh, I'm sorry, I'm getting riled up about Fask and what I wanted to do was tell you *thank you*. For taking care of Dalaya. For taking care of *me*." What he really wanted to do was kiss her.

"Dalaya did most of the heavy lifting," Mackenzie said, blushing. "I'm...just..."

"You're not *just* anything," Kenth said warmly.

She was standing so close to him now, and Kenth could

feel complicated *new* things from her, fresh and immediate. Trust. Affection. Attraction.

If he were one of his smoother brothers, he'd know what to say to win her. He wanted to touch her, because he knew she wanted his touch, but wanting wasn't the same as asking, and he wasn't sure that begging her would help his cause.

"Mackenzie..." he started, just as she said, "I wish..."

"Tell me," Kenth encouraged swiftly.

"Don't you know?" Mackenzie said plaintively.

"I can't tell your thoughts," he reminded her. "Only your emotions. Your...*feelings.*" His voice went gruff on the last word, his implication clear.

"I wish I knew what *you* were feeling," she said, and Kenth could hear her frustration as well as he could feel it. "I wish I had you in my mind, that I didn't have to guess everything and could just...believe." She drew in a sharp breath and laughed. "I lived my whole life in a place where we were trained to believe without question and here I am now in a place that is all questions. What do you want for dinner, what would you like to do now, where would you like to go? No one ever gave me choices before."

Then she lifted her chin.

"I choose you," she said boldly, and Kenth was awed by the courage that he could tell it took. She was still holding his gaze, though her hands twisted together uncomfortably. "You already know that I want you."

"Knowing what you want isn't the same as consent," he reminded her, struggling for the high ground. "And you've been drinking."

She laughed warmly. "Only soda. Anything stronger seemed...imprudent."

Kenth smiled because she was so refreshingly sensible. "Do you *want* me to kiss you?"

The rush of her desire was a clear answer, but Kenth still waited for her whispered, "Yes…"

He gathered her into his arms as slowly as he could manage, not wanting to frighten her, giving her every chance to protest as he took her face in one hand and slipped the other around her waist to draw her close.

He kissed her so gently that he could barely feel her against his lips. It was like trying to tame a wild bird to his hand. She was so frightened and so brave and she wanted him so much.

He backed his mouth off after the barest touch.

"I can't share what I'm feeling here." Kenth tapped her forehead and then let his fingers fall to her lips. "But I can share it here. I can show you." Her breath was hot over his thumb and he let it rest there as an invitation.

Then his mouth was on hers and Kenth forgot to be slow and soft, fired by how much she liked it and how ready she was to respond to his touch. She let him press her up against the wall of the hallway and opened her mouth for his tongue hungrily. The combination of his body's response, and hers, and the strength of emotion resonating through their mate bond was almost too much to bear.

He had to force himself to gentleness, not wanting to frighten her, and that rose a swell of tenderness behind her hot need that made Kenth feel like a giant or a god.

"Mackenzie," he breathed when he was able to pull his mouth from hers. "Mackenzie, I love you."

Her eyes gleamed suspiciously, and Kenth realized that he'd never told her that, and she wouldn't have felt that truth from the mate bond like he did. He could tell what hearing the words did for her, and vowed to repeat it every day until he died. "I love you. I *love* you."

CHAPTER 20

"You might…" Mackenzie tried to protest. "It's just a possibility."

"Not I *will* love you, not I *might* love you," Kenth told her firmly. "I *love* you. It doesn't matter what the Compact thinks, it doesn't even matter that I know what you think. I've watched you be braver than any prince or dragon I've ever known. I've fought at your side. I've seen how gentle and patient you are with my daughter and the other kids. You're smart, and funny, and kind. You saved me, and you won my heart, fair and square. Just you."

The best part about the mate bond is that he knew he'd said the right thing by the way that she softened inside, the way her reservations crumbled away.

When he kissed her again, it was as soft as his first one, just a promise of a kiss, the brush of lip on lip.

"They're expecting us at dinner," Mackenzie said shyly, but Kenth suspected that dinner was the last place she really wanted to go.

Kenth remembered Leinani's smirk, Carina's laughter, and Tania's knowing look. "They aren't *really* expecting us," he told Mackenzie confidently. "We could have food brought to my room later."

She looked at him, wide-eyed, as she realized what he meant.

"If you want," he added swiftly. "Only if you want."

He felt her conflict ease and fade to nothing as she put her hand into his. "I'm doing all the bold things today," she said trustingly. "Why not this, too?"

Ours, only ours, Kenth's dragon sang.

CHAPTER 21

Mackenzie wasn't sure what made everything fall into place so perfectly.

Part of it was being buoyed up by the unexpected and inclusive kindness of the princesses. Part of it was the general relief that was so thick in the castle. Some of it was that this place and the people who lived here were wearing down the armor of distance that she had always worn to protect herself. She was finally convinced that the children were going to be kept safe, that they weren't going to be tossed to the wolves because they were all painfully inconvenient.

And most of it was Kenth himself.

He was so kind and generous and *safe*.

The other mates had spoken about how the spell had made them feel protected, like their prince was a haven in a storm, and Mackenzie couldn't help but wonder if they weren't *forced* to that feeling.

But there was no magic making *her* trust *Kenth*. Only his loyalty and devotion, his actions louder than any projected emotions, could make her believe the truth of him.

He loved her.

And when he said it, looking into her eyes, kissing her with that mouth, Mackenzie believed it.

That was his truth.

Did she love him in return? He said that she would, and she didn't doubt that she could. But was this fire that he kindled in her now really love or only fondness and desire? She had the craziest crush on him, she had to admit, but how much of that was projecting all of her favorite book heroes onto him?

There was certainly no denying her desire. Not now, hurrying hand-in-hand down the hall to his rooms. They passed Dalaya's door, hearing muffled sounds of her play with Mrs. James within, and went on to his sitting room, where Kenth closed the door behind them and paused to look searchingly at her.

"Are you sure?" he said.

He was so careful with her, so deliberate in giving her choices and freedom. Did he know what it did to her to be considered the driver of her own destiny, not just a simple pawn in someone else's larger game? It was terrifying and tremendous and he had to know every complicated emotion that it sparked in her.

"I'm sure," she said. This was Kenth, and he loved her, and the only thing she had to offer was herself...and somehow he wanted that. He wanted *her*.

And she wanted him right back.

Like the other mates said, why shouldn't they?

She didn't wait for his kiss this time, but stood up on tip-toe and pulled his face down to hers.

She wasn't a virgin, but all of her previous encounters, awkward and hungry, had been about her body, never about her heart.

This was about all of her: her whole soul, all of her

trust, her entire self. She wanted him, desperately. She wanted to try all of the impossible acts she'd read about, each in succession, until she was screaming for release.

He hissed near her ear and Mackenzie wondered if he could feel how worked up she was. Was *lust* an emotion? She could feel his cock, because she was pressing herself against him, but she wasn't sure how much of his excitement was the echo of hers. Could he tell where she stopped and he began? Did magic muddle this all up too much?

Would he still want her without the spell?

His hands were at neck, cradling her face so he could kiss her deeply, tracing the lines of her jaw and he drew back then and looked deeply into her eyes. It was every bit as intense as romance books said it would be, he was so close and so *raw*. "Mackenzie," he said gruffly. "Mackenzie, you are my heart."

There were sweet nothings that were probably appropriate for such a moment, but Mackenzie's head was blank with hunger. She just knew that she wanted more of him, she wanted that awe-inspiring chest that she'd seen when he first woke up from his poisoned sleep, and she wanted those big arms bare around her. "More, please, more," she begged.

To her delight and relief, he swept her up into his arms then, as if he knew what she was thinking and not just what she was feeling, and took her through the door to his bedroom.

It was not at all the same sorrow-filled room that it had been while he was dying. The air was fresh and the curtains were open wide to a stunning sunset over snow-covered trees.

He laid her down on the bed and leaned over to kiss her, which proved to be even more fun than kissing standing up, and Mackenzie thought that his weight on her, being pinned in his embrace, was more exciting than anything she'd ever read. She got her hands up under his shirt, and he gave a gargle of pleasure and need when she clawed at his back to draw him even closer.

He got one hand around to the back of her head and kissed her harder than ever. Mackenzie kissed him back just as urgently. How could kisses even be like this? The muscles around her mouth were aching, but she only wanted more and more. His tongue was in her mouth, which was the kind of thing she'd read and imagined, but never imagined would be like *this*. How much of him could she take? How much of himself could he give?

They were still wearing clothing, and it felt like a terrible shame that there was anything between them but skin. When Kenth sat up rather suddenly to shuck off his shirt, Mackenzie's breath caught in her throat because even making out with him with the burning memory of his handsome shirtless self in her head was not equal to real sight of him now, broad-chested and beautiful.

He was her prince. Her dragon prince.

And he was unbuttoning her shirt.

He had slowed down again, and Mackenzie licked her sore lips and wondered how he even managed buttons. She felt incredibly clumsy, as if her whole body was so keenly wound up that all her signals were getting crossed. When the cool air touched the skin at the top of her breasts, she felt like every single nerve was singing. And when he touched her, reverently, there was suddenly a chorus.

He paused when he slid the sleeves from her arm, ever so slightly, and his fingers trailed over the tattoo on her forearm.

She was marked with his enemy's icon. Would that matter?

He finished pulling off her sleeve and didn't linger there.

She was on fire, between her legs, at the very core of her soul, even as goosebumps rose on the skin that Kenth uncovered.

"Are you cold?" he asked, tracing between her breasts.

"I am so very hot," Mackenzie said, and she only heard how foolish it sounded after she spoke.

They laughed together, because they couldn't help it, and because laughter was a release of the tension that was eating them both alive. "You are very hot," he agreed, pulling her up to a sitting position so he could reach behind her and tease her bra loose. "Very, very, *very* hot."

Mackenzie confused herself pulling the bra off of her shoulders and when she had figured out her limbs again, she could not keep from putting her hands on that gorgeous expanse of chest. "It's definitely mutual," she said in awe as she spread her fingers and slid them to his shoulders. "You are…wow. Very, very, *very* wow."

She knew what happened next and when Kenth stood to unclasp his pants, she scrambled up too, slipping her jeans off with a thrill of anticipation. She left her underwear on, then wasn't sure she should have, because Kenth was stepping out of his pants completely naked, his cock hard before him. He found a condom in a bedside drawer and rolled it on.

Mackenzie was just wondering if she should take her underwear off herself when Kenth threw back the comforter on his bed and drew her down into the smooth sheets. He held her against him, letting her get used to the feel of him pressing at her vulva with the flimsy protection of her underwear. Mackenzie was whimpering, she realized, wordlessly begging him for more.

Then she was glad that she'd left her underwear on,

because she got the pleasure of having them slipped off of her by Kenth, cupping her ass as he pulled them down, slowly stroking down her legs as he released them from her feet one by one.

Then, rather than covering her again as he had when he kissed her, he rolled onto his back and pulled her up to straddle him.

It gave her a position of power, holding herself right at his cock. His hands were at her hips, holding her, but not holding her back or forcing her down. She gazed at him, at the beautiful planes of his shoulders, at the perfect lines of his dear, dear face, at the dark hair of his chest, the tense muscles in his neck as he panted and waited for her to make the first move.

He made an animal noise as Mackenzie finally lowered herself, taking him inch by careful inch, until she thought she could take no more, she was so exquisitely full and everything was perfect.

She couldn't define the moment that they started moving together, only knew that they were, slowly at first, then harder and faster, in a blur of carnal pleasure. Would he feel it in his mind when she came? Mackenzie only had a moment to wonder before she was pitching off a wave of release so sharp and fulfilling that she didn't realize she was crying out.

Spent, she lowered herself down on him, kissing his neck as the aftermath shuddered through her. He wrapped his arms tight around her, holding her through every echo of bliss, before rolling with her so that he was covering her, entering her even deeper than before.

There was no wondering when he came, clutching at her, making noises of need, desperately erratic at the end after being so deliberate and careful with her. Did she imagine that she could feel his pleasure, like the tickle his feelings at the edge of her senses?

At the end of it all, Mackenzie laughed out loud, because she was so full of happiness and joy.

"I'm crushing you," Kenth said, and his laughter in her ear as he fell over on his side without letting go of her was as much a reward as her own release.

"I love you crushing me," Mackenzie said honestly, and her laughter stilled as she heard her own words, and felt them in her heart. *I love you...* He couldn't hear the thoughts and she wasn't brave enough to say it out loud, not by itself.

Sex was one milestone enough. She felt too blissful to pursue another, with all the tangled and uncertain expectations that might come with it.

CHAPTER 22

After a brief shower together, Kenth wrapped Mackenzie in his oversized robe, kissed her, and texted for food.

"My lips hurt," she complained happily, curling up on his couch while he got dressed.

"*All* of them?" Kenth wanted to know, with a suggestive waggle of his eyebrows.

She giggled and blushed and made a show of looking down her bathrobe. "*All* of them," she confirmed.

Probably that shouldn't make him feel as good as it did, but she felt so deeply content in his head, as relaxed and full of joy as she had ever been and Kenth loved that he could play some role in that. She was always taking on the weight of responsibilities that she didn't deserve to carry and he was glad to see her enjoying the moment.

A curt text from Mrs. James reminded him that he wasn't the only prince in the castle, and if he wasn't willing to show up for meals, he could wait and it wouldn't be hot.

Kenth deleted an eggplant emoji and texted her back a

blowing heart. "It might be a while before we get food service," he warned Mackenzie.

She shrugged, and some of her happiness dampened. "We sometimes had to wait a long time for food," she said. "Amara said that suffering *heightened* appreciation."

Kenth would have done anything to take that suffering from her and he didn't realize that he was scowling at her until he felt the little prickle of her guilt for ruining the moment. "It's not your fault," he said gruffly. "Nothing Amara did is your fault."

"I know," Mackenzie said, and Kenth felt a curious tingle of it in their bond. She didn't entirely believe it yet, but she was starting to, like new roots taking hold in fertile soil.

"I've got plans for you," Kenth warned her.

To his delight, she glanced back at the bed. "Plans, you say?"

He laughed and had to kiss her then because those seemed like the best possible plans. He drew back after only a moment.

"You don't have to stop," she begged. "My lips don't hurt that badly. Not any of them…"

"I'm going to show you how to have fun," Kenth said, leaving one final kiss on her nose.

"Didn't you *just* do that?" Mackenzie teased.

"Oh, there's more where that came from," Kenth promised. "But I'm talking about *Plan Fun*. I'm going to teach you how to ice skate. We're going to have snowball fights and tea parties. I'm going to show you classic movies. We're going to play all the games."

"I know a few card games," Mackenzie said. "But I've always wanted to play Monopoly. So many books reference it, and I've never been able to figure out how it works."

"We're going to play Monopoly," Kenth declared. "And

Battleship, and Scrabble, and Mario Brothers. I'll teach you beer pong! Everything normal. Everything you've ever missed."

He was not, perhaps, the *best* person to show Mackenzie how to have fun, but he had never been so inspired to do anything in his life. "Let's start now."

"Right now?" Mackenzie giggled. "This very moment?"

"I can think of no better time. Let's go collect what we need from Dalaya's room."

It was nearly an hour before Mrs. James texted him that there was a tray coming up, and the maid, an unfamiliar face, sensibly knocked and did not come in until Kenth called, "Enter!"

If it surprised her to find them sitting on the floor playing Sorry! in their bathrobes with an excited and up-past-her-bedtime Dalaya, she professionally didn't give any indication of it.

"That was only six squares, Sweetheart," Kenth pointed out. "Go one more!"

"Slide!" Dalaya squealed in joy.

"Ahhhh!" Mackenzie cried. "You knocked me back to Start!"

They ate their sandwiches and chips at the coffee table, Kenth sitting close to Dalaya to wipe her hands before she took cards or moved pieces. The game was close to the very end and Mackenzie came from behind for a triumphant win that Kenth felt to his toes.

"I'm not tired!" Dalaya said, as soon as she saw Kenth putting the game pieces away, but she pouted and rubbed her eyes in a dead giveaway.

"Bathtime!" he said, sweeping her up into his arms and giving her a little toss.

It was as swift a bath as possible with Dalaya dragging

her feet at every step, but Mackenzie was a cheerful distraction. Kenth thought like everything was exactly, perfectly as it ought to be. He was safe in his family home with his mate and his daughter, in rooms filled with laughter.

Despite continuing to insist that she wasn't sleepy, Dalaya was unconscious almost the moment her head hit her pillow. Mackenzie and Kenth crept away with their hands over their mouths to keep from giggling out loud.

"How is Plan Fun going?" Kenth wanted to know, drawing her into his arms when the door to his sitting room was closed behind them.

"I like the first stage of the plan a lot," Mackenzie said, her eyes sparkling. "What's next?"

Kenth answered with a kiss, long and lingering. "What else have you always wanted to do?"

"Music," she said promptly. "We never had music in the Cause and I read so much about the power it has. What's jazz? And punk? It's supposed to be music of the revolution."

Kenth didn't have much music, but he could download albums on his phone and play them on a little blue tooth speaker. Mackenzie was disappointed in the jazz that he found on a random Internet search and baffled by the punk, but wildly enthusiastic about country.

"It's so...plaintive," she said.

Kenth vowed to learn to love it, because she enjoyed it so much. And he certainly didn't object to making love *to* it, peeling her out of the bathrobe and laying her down to find anew all the sensitive parts of her skin to kiss and caress.

She fell asleep before he did, sated and exhausted, and Kenth watched her for a long while, marveling at the peace in her face, and the soft strawberry-blond waves of her hair over the pillow.

~

The following day dawned brilliant but late, turning the forest into a fluffy haven of blue shadows. It was cold, as it often was when it was clear, and there was a new dust of sparkling dry snow over everything.

Kenth read his texts from Fask, turned off his phone, bundled Mackenzie and Dalaya into coats, and dragged them out into the snow for more of *Plan Fun*.

"Is that a toboggan?" Mackenzie exclaimed when they got outside. She sensibly wrapped her scarf tight around her and pulled her hat down over her ears.

"No one calls them that anymore," Kenth told her kindly.

"It's a *sled*," Dalaya explained confidently, clambering in without invitation. "Pull me! Pull me, Daddy!"

"Am I pulling you, too?" Kenth offered Mackenzie.

She looked like she wasn't sure he was serious and shook her head. "I can walk," she assured him.

The trails that crisscrossed the property had been freshly groomed and were wide and smooth. Dalaya shrieked with joy as Kenth broke into a run, pulling her so fast that she fell back in the sled. Mackenzie bounded after them, laughing.

He slowed so that she could keep up. The trails wound up into the hills and back down and all three of them piled in for the downslopes, frequently missing the curves and turns to crash, unconcerned, into the fluffy banks on either side.

The first time they nosed off the trail into the snow,

both Dalaya and Mackenzie were alarmed and then quiet with hesitation as they struggled back to the hard-packed surface. The second time, Kenth crashed them on purpose. By the third, all three of them were laughing out loud and leaning wildly for the deepest banks.

The creak of skis warned Kenth as he pulled Dalaya to the top of a blind corner and he got the sled over to the side just in time for Tray to come streaking past at the heels of two of his dogs, Shayla and Dusty.

"On by!" Tray cried. "On by!"

He was on skis, and Leinani came shortly after, looking only marginally more in control with just one dog. "Woah, Tanana," she said desperately. "Woah, this thing doesn't have reins! Woah!" She flailed her ski poles.

Tanana, clearly divided between obedience and following Tray and her hellbent littermates, was distracted when Dalaya gave a squeal of greeting and decided that going over to lick the little girl's face was the best of both worlds.

This led inevitably to a tangle of the sled lines and Leinani's skijoring lead.

Kenth and Mackenzie were still chortling and untying them when Tray got himself and his two turned around and appeared around the corner again.

"Hello niece!" he called to Dalaya.

"I'm snowy!" she replied, falling backward into the sled with hysterical giggles.

This was utterly irresistible to Tanana, who charged forward to try to climb in after her and lick her face. Caught by surprise, Leinani was yanked directly into Kenth and only dragon reflexes kept them both upright as she hollered in vain, "Tanana, no!"

Kenth was unreasonably pleased by Mackenzie's brief stab of jealousy.

CHAPTER 22

"No, Shayla! No, Dusty! Leave it!" Tray called when they wanted to dive into the fray, quivering from nose to tail with canine desire. He couldn't assist at all, more interested in keeping his own dogs back. They danced in place, whining and yipping, but obediently stayed back while Tray leaned on his ski poles and laughed unhelpfully.

Shayla lay down on her side and rolled in the snow, kicking her bootied paws in the air. Leinani once again unclipped her lead and got Tanana untangled from the sled ropes and pulled off the giggling Dalaya, who was not helping matters at all by wrestling whole-heartedly with the dog and hugging everything she could reach.

At last, they were all separated, Dalaya sitting in the sled, Leinani pulling away with Tanana looking wistfully over her shoulder.

"Going to do the big slope?" Tray asked with a waggle of his eyebrows.

"Is it clear?" Kenth asked in return, aware of Mackenzie watching him curiously.

"Toren and Carina took the kids out yesterday. Might be a little new powder down on it, but it should be plenty fast."

Kenth could feel the cold on his teeth, he was grinning so wide.

"Have fun," Tray said merrily. "Let's go, Shayla! Let's go, Dusty! Go catch Leinani and Tanana!"

They surged eagerly forward, tongues flapping, and Tray skied expertly after them. He waved one skipole back at them as Dalaya sat up in the sled and wiggled her mitten forlornly after them.

"What's the big slope?" Mackenzie asked suspiciously.

"It's just ahead," Kenth promised. "You're all warmed up for it."

"I'm cold," Dalaya complained. Her cheeks were rosy red and her nose was running.

Kenth checked her temperature with his hands. "You good for one last sled run?" he asked. "It takes us back in the direction of home anyway."

"She can take my scarf," Mackenzie offered. "I'm not cold."

"You ought to be," Kenth observed, but he wasn't all that great at judging temperatures; his dragon kept him from being bothered by extreme cold or heat. "Where's your hat?"

Mackenzie put a startled hand to her head. "I must have lost it!" she said in laughing astonishment. Her cheeks were red, too, but Kenth thought it was more from her warm thoughts about him than it was from cold. She took her scarf off and wrapped it around Dalaya's neck, enough times that only the little girl's dancing eyes were visible and her giggles were muffled.

"Let's go," Mackenzie said. "We can all warm up back at the castle!"

She trotted beside him, mittened hand in his as Dalaya rolled around in the sled behind them. A pair of ravens dove and offered croaking opinions, and a swarm of finches chirped their joy for the sunshine and seeds.

It wasn't far to the top of what Kenth and his brothers had always called The Big Slope.

"I see why you call it that," Mackenzie said, gazing down the open grade. "Is it safe?"

It was hard to tell how high they had climbed through the forest until they got to this view. It was a long way down the steep sled run, the lake at the bottom a white, flat disc. They couldn't see the castle from here, just the snow-covered forest hills past the frozen lake, and the craggy mountains beyond them.

Kenth positioned the sled at the crest. "We've been sledding this hill since I was younger than Dalaya," he said comfortingly. Mackenzie stepped close to get into the sled and Kenth took her unintentional proximity to steal a kiss that she gladly leaned into. Her lips were warm against him, but he still pulled up the hood of her jacket and drew it close. "I'll keep you safe," he promised.

"Go, go, go!" Dalaya cried eagerly.

Mackenzie slipped into the sled behind her, her feet on either side of the little girl and her arms wrapped tight around her shoulders. "I don't know," she said, but she said it with cheer and Kenth could feel her eager anticipation. "This is not a plaaaaan!"

Kenth kicked them off and scrambled in last, legs and limbs barely fitting, so that Mackenzie was tight up in his arms and he could reach around to hold Dalaya as they picked up speed down the drop.

Dalaya shrieked in joy and Mackenzie gave an involuntary squeal that turned into a cry of joy as they rocketed down the slope so fast that tears rose in his eyes. He hadn't been sledding in years, but he remembered how to lean into the curves, guiding them down off the shallow jump that made both of his passengers give little screams as they briefly soared through the air. They landed with a harmless thump and gradually slowed as the snow leveled below them.

"More, more, more!" Dalaya cried, laughing and struggling in their arms.

For a long moment, Kenth could only hold them both close in a perfect space of happiness as the sled finally came to a stop.

"We should go back home," Mackenzie said regretfully, leaning her head back on Kenth's shoulder. He could just kiss her at the side of the mouth and couldn't resist doing so.

He looked up to catch Dalaya's curious gaze as she wriggled from their grip and tried to crawl out of the sled. She managed to topple out head first and was so thoroughly insulated that she had trouble getting her feet back under her. "Help!" she laughed, and Kenth recognized the tired note to her voice.

He and Mackenzie got up out of the sled and Kenth swept Dalaya up into his arms, then led them across the lake back towards the castle, one hand in Mackenzie's, dragging the empty sled behind them.

Only as the grand building came into sight did he recognize that Mackenzie had called it *home.*

It felt completely natural.

CHAPTER 23

"*Plan Fun* is going to have to wait a bit today," Kenth told her, a few mornings later.

Mackenzie sleepily stretched, reveling in the smooth sheets and the perfect pillow and the afterglow of Kenth's morning lovemaking. She knew it was only her own imagination, but she thought she could feel a hum of Kenth in her mind, like a strum of music that completed her. She was so comfortable that she thought she might even go back to sleep until Kenth finished whatever royal business Fask was foisting on him. "Have fun!"

His next words brought her immediately up to a sitting position: "Fask is ready to let you look at the Compact."

Mackenzie was wide awake now.

She had already looked over the handful of spells that Amara had accidentally left at the site of one of her attempts at the Compact, and she had successfully answered all of their questions. "The spell that makes a chair sprout fur is a result of exhaustion," she explained with a frown. "Amara drove them too hard." She confirmed that Amara had many of the spells set to end with the command, "Alto!"

She was relieved by how well the children had settled in and how much they had blossomed with the affection and resources of the castle. She was almost sad about how little they needed her now, but was glad to see them pursuing their own interests and pleasures. They leaned on each other with a tight-knit camaraderie that suggested that it might be challenging to separate them even if they ever did find their proper families.

Fask activated one of the spells, as a test of her gift, and Mackenzie was relieved when it did exactly as she predicted.

These were properly structured spells, if somewhat juvenile in execution, and they had logical patterns that she could see in the mirrored vault of her own mind.

She scrambled to shower and dress, eager to see what was generally agreed to be the most complicated magical item ever created.

When Kenth unlocked the vault with his name, Mackenzie was staggered by the magic potentials within. The door was steeped in protections and the rock that the vault itself was in was shot through with intentions. There was a dagger in a stand at the center of the glittering hoard that made Mackenzie's skin crawl; it reminded her of the flavor of the magic that had hurt Kenth. There was an etched glass bottle that would draw drink from far away with the proper request, and a mirror that would show a single perfect memory.

And all of it dulled compared to the Compact.

Mackenzie had seen a lot of spells over the years. Not just the sloppy, spell-driven magic pages of the children they had rescued from Amara, but artifacts and heirloom spells like Leinani's listening rings. Amara had amassed a number of powerful weapons and useful tools.

But she had never been in the presence of something like the Compact.

She went unerringly to it, though that was perhaps unsurprising, because it was featured on a center table, with all of the most magical and powerful items, and she forgot that Fask was even with them until he hissed in outrage. "Don't *touch* it!"

Mackenzie looked at him blankly, her brain so full of *this-then-that* and dazzling possibilities that she didn't even really register him.

"It's so…complicated," she said in awe. The hollow place inside of her was singing, like it had hit some kind of resonance.

Most magical items did one thing, and they did it very simply, with one activation and one way to end it. It took so much concentration to make a thing happen with magic that there was no reward in making it more complex without strict necessity; if you needed a spell to do two things, there was no reason not to simply have two spells.

This…this was like standing in the middle of a rushing river or a tornado of music. There were melodies everywhere, overlapping. She was astonished by the number of options, the possible outcomes. Everything was interlocking, every step was driven by the step before. It wasn't just a powerful spell, it was a *machine*. Every other spell she'd ever seen dwindled in meaning. The most elegant artifacts were reduced to wind-up cymbal-clapping monkeys compared to a car or a symphony. A car that was a symphony. A symphony that spanned time.

She didn't even have to go into the place in her mind where she usually saw spells, it was already reaching out to her.

It was more than a treaty, more than a recital of rules or a structure for a society. It was like a program with infinite endings. It could do…anything. And this was only a tiny piece of it…

"Mackenzie?"

She could barely hear Kenth's voice, full of concern, over the noise in her head.

"What can it do?" Fask demanded. "What do you see?"

"No wonder Amara wants it," she said breathlessly. "I have never felt power like this in my life. I didn't know that kind of power was possible. It's so *beautiful.*"

"What could she do with it?" Fask wanted to know. When Mackenzie didn't reply at once, gazing blankly through him, he gave her shoulder a little shake.

"Don't touch her," Kenth snarled at him, wedging himself between them forcefully.

Mackenzie closed her eyes, barely registering Fask's touch or their clash.

She went to the empty place inside of her, expecting it to take some time for the reflections of something so complex to line up and start to make sense, and discovered that she was not alone in the space.

There was a woman there with her, an old woman with a cloak like ink and hair like spun silver.

"Who are you?" Mackenzie asked anxiously. This had never happened before.

The woman didn't answer, only smiled slyly. "Have you ever noticed that if you are in a bright room during a dark night, a window can look like a mirror?"

Mackenzie stared at her. "I suppose I have."

"When you turn the light off, you can see things you couldn't before."

"Who are you?" Mackenzie repeated. "How are you in my head like this?"

The old woman shook her head, and her silver hair floated from her like dandelion fluff. "You haven't figured it out yet?"

No one had ever been in this space where Mackenzie saw magic. Not Amara, not Kenth. She'd thought it was her own imagination, her brain trying to make sense of her gift. But this was something from outside of herself, something bigger, something terrifyingly strong.

This was where she came to unravel spells, to sense their potentials like she was a bat using sonar to bounce off a wall. Her inner mirror let her see magic here.

And the woman *was* magic. *Entirely* magic.

"You're the Compact," Mackenzie realized in astonishment.

The woman slow-clapped. "Now you're putting it together."

Mackenzie stared. The Compact was so enormous and complex that it had become…real. It—she!—was self-aware in a way no spell she'd ever seen could possibly be, like a computer program that had inadvertently outgrown its code to become an artificial intelligence.

Or maybe not inadvertently.

What was it that Amara said about dragons? They were the bridge between magic and mundane. They were the evil demons that kept mortals from wielding magic.

Understanding shot through Mackenzie like a lightning bolt.

The Compact was not just a treaty between countries for trade concerns and successions. It wasn't just land and money and petty mundane concerns with a little magical enforcement. The Compact was what kept magic itself from descending into chaos. It was the *structure* of structured magic itself.

"You hold the bridge," Mackenzie said in awe.

"I *am* the bridge," the Compact corrected.

Mackenzie remembered her real purpose through the wonder. "Some of the pages, they've been stolen. I was supposed to see if that had damaged it—ah, you?"

"I am dying," the Compact said frankly.

"Dying?" Mackenzie had only just met her but was already appalled by the idea. And if she did… She gazed at the reflections in her space, horrified by the mirror-possibilities if the Compact failed.

"All spells fade. I have died and been Renewed many times." The Compact stepped forward and Mackenzie felt her hands, rough like sandpaper, against her cheeks. "You are going to be fine," she said kindly. "The hardest part is yet to come, but you will see clearly at last when the time is right. I've arranged as much as I can and I have other kingdoms to watch over." She laughed wryly. "And *I* have to follow my own rules."

There was a curious emphasis on *I*.

Then she dissolved into a flock of ravens made of galaxies that made Mackenzie flinch away in reflex and was gone.

CHAPTER 24

"Mackenzie? Are you alright?" Kenth was holding her up, which was good, because it seemed as though she had forgotten which direction was up.

"I'm okay, I'm okay!" she insisted. "I saw it. I understand it. Oh, it's..." she laughed then, sagging weakly into Kenth. "She's real. She's alive."

"Who? Who is?" Kenth wanted to know. "Are you sure you're okay?"

"Who is alive?" Fask demanded.

Mackenzie seemed to remember she had legs and was able to stand again. "The Compact. She's not *just* a spell. Not even just a really complicated one. She's aware, and curious, and...kind."

"She?" Fask said skeptically.

"She looked like an old woman with white hair."

"Our castle spirit?" Kenth said incredulously.

He and Fask exchanged dubious looks.

"I thought she was a ghost," Fask said.

"She's not a ghost," Mackenzie said firmly. "She's a *spell*, and she's dying."

"What do you mean, dying?" Fask asked between gritted teeth.

"All spells fade," Mackenzie reminded him. She shook her head. "The Renewal, no wonder Amara wanted to stop it. Oh, everything makes sense now."

"Not to me, it doesn't," Fask said impatiently. "Did the stolen pages mean it's been harmed?"

"Not it. *She*," Mackenzie insisted. "She said that she had died and been Renewed many times. She didn't seem bothered by the missing pages. She is nearly at the end of her cycle and I think it matters less now?"

She looked at Kenth and blinked, looking for all of the world like she was trying to translate something. "It's a lot to understand, but let me try to explain. It's…imagine most spells as a program, written out with exacting code full of if/thens, limited to the possibilities the programmer anticipates. We're not much different, you know. We react to stimuli, we are programmed by our experiences and by the media we input into our systems. A spell like this, so complicated, is like an artificial intelligence, just as complex and real. It's—she's!—made the leap to being alive, at some point."

Mackenzie was excited by the idea, and eager to share.

"There's always been an understanding that there's a difference between structured magic and natural. Natural magic is specific talents, with specific limits. Shapeshifting, cloaking, garden magic. It doesn't take a spell, and it's something you're born with. That energy comes from this world, like a well of water. But there's another world, just off from ours, and the magic from that world can fuel another kind of magic, what we call structured magic. It can be put into motion using spells, following strict rules.

They have to be written with intention, only by someone who can maintain the appropriate focus."

"The Compact told you all of that?" Fask said skeptically.

"Not exactly," Mackenzie said. The Compact seemed to have filled her with courage; she didn't seem the slighted bit cowed by Fask's doubt. "Some of this information comes from old documents about magic, some of it from… Amara's experiments. The Compact confirmed a few guesses for me."

"Where do dragons fit in this?" Kenth wanted to know. "They've never seemed entirely structured magic or natural."

"They are natural, but not to this world," Mackenzie said. Her eyes were full of wonder. "They are like…a door between our worlds. This is why spells can have longer strength and duration when Amara controls one—it's a little like opening a tap all the way."

"Faerie?" Kenth guessed. "The other world is like faerie?"

Fask made a snorting noise but Mackenzie was nodding. "I mean, that's a gross simplification. It's a place of magic, a whole plane of power."

"It doesn't sound like such a bad thing," Fask suggested. "Opening the taps, I mean."

Kenth's dragon gave a shiver of disapproval.

What do you think of all of this? Kenth asked him.

We guard the bridge, came the cryptic answer. The dragon didn't always have feelings that matched up with human emotion, much like he didn't have memories quite like Kenth did, but he was definitely disturbed by this information. Fask didn't seem bothered; maybe his own dragon didn't object to it.

"Where does the Compact fit into this?" Fask asked.

"The Compact doesn't just follow the rules of magic," Mackenzie said. "It *is* the rules. Without it, *all* magic would be wild, it would *all* be chaos." She frowned. "Amara must think that without the Compact, she would have control over all that power, but she wouldn't. No one can. It would fly out of control. The world would burn."

"You're saying that if the Compact *isn't* Renewed, it's the end of the world?"

For once, Kenth didn't blame Fask for sounding cross.

Mackenzie nodded. "This is why she's so hellbent on stealing the Compact, and why she's trying to eliminate and undermine the royalty. It's not just political instability that she wants. She wants the Renewal to not happen at all. She could destroy the pages of the Compact, or she could capture or kill the dragons necessary to renew it. Either would ensure that the Renewal didn't occur."

"All this time, I thought Amara just didn't *like* us," Kenth said dryly.

Fask considered. "Well, can we just tell her that this is a bad idea? I mean, the destruction of the world is in no one's favor."

Trust Fask to think there was a diplomatic solution.

"She's a madwoman," Mackenzie said with a frown. "I wish that logic would work on her, but I know that it won't. She has the scent of power and is unlikely to let the trail go cold."

"Can't the Compact just…I don't know, snap her into line?" Kenth wanted to know.

"The Compact said she has to follow her own rules," Mackenzie observed. "I felt like maybe she was constrained by something."

"This is a conversation that should be continued with the others," Fask said firmly. "Not down here in the vault.

After lunch, we'll get everyone together. Mackenzie, will you join us?"

Kenth felt her joy at being invited, but she accepted very gravely, no hint of the pride that she felt in her face or voice. "I would love to, thank you." She would be a magnificent diplomat, Kenth thought, with just a modicum more of self-confidence.

She would be a magnificent *queen*.

CHAPTER 25

"I'm never sure why I'm asked to come to these things," Carina said near Mackenzie's ear. "I mean, Tania, she's super smart, and she practically has the Compact memorized, and Leinani has all the princess training and personally has rubbed elbows with the royalty of every single Small Kingdoms country, but I'm the dumb American over here like 'What's a treaty, again?'"

Mackenzie couldn't help but giggle nervously. She'd been seated far down the table, between Kenth and Carina, and the mood was very different from the casual meals they took in the same room. Each seat was laid out with an agenda, a pen, and a glass of water. Toren was folding a paper airplane out of his program just past Carina.

"I'm not sure why I'm here, either," Drayger said from across the table in a stage whisper. "I'm never sure if I'm honored guest, irritating prisoner, or valuable inside knowledge."

Captain Luke, sitting at the end of the table, was happy to clarify, "Irritating prisoner."

Fask scowled as Raval came in with a mumbled apology and took the last seat. But then, Fask had been scowling a lot since their visit to the vault to see the Compact.

"If you're all quite finished?" Fask said coolly, glaring down the table.

The various hushed conversations died away, and Carina waved an informal apology.

"Thank you for your prompt attendance," Fask said, with a pointed look at Raval. "We've got a lot to cover and a few new problems to address. I've made a list and want to get through this quickly, so we aren't spending all day here. I'm sure you all have more interesting things to do."

Mackenzie glanced at the page curiously. It was organized in a formal outline, and the first topic was current affairs.

A painting on the wall behind Fask proved to be a television screen and he had a small remote that he used to bring up an image of newspaper headlines and Internet screenshots.

They started somewhat innocuously, with reports in mainstream media about unexplained phenomena and unexpected sightings. Major and respected newspapers speculated about things that couldn't be explained by science and weren't being claimed by major religions.

"Casters and shifters are getting sloppy," Fask observed. "Or magic is getting more chaotic. We'll return to this in a few moments."

The slides moved on to topics that were all quite grim, and the mood of the room chilled considerably. Protests, complaints about Small Kingdoms rule, assassination attempts.

Bold among them was the headline that the King and Queen of Majorca had been killed in a car wreck. There was no hint of murder, but everyone at the table was considering the likelihood.

"Well, shit," Drayger said with a dry laugh. "I guess I know why I'm here *now*."

Mackenzie eyed Fask. It was callous of him to spring this kind of news on Drayger without warning, even if the Majorcan prince was a bastard son who wasn't close to his blood parent. Did Fask hope to surprise a reaction out of him? Amara had handled every bit of information like a weapon, and that was the kind of thing she might do.

"Are you in line to inherit?" Tray asked.

"Maybe ninth," Drayger said. "Dad and I were definitely not close, and he's got three legitimate sons before anything falls to me."

"Does one of them have a mate?" Fask asked pointedly. "Because the Renewal is coming up fast, and it's...a lot more important than we realized."

Drayger didn't notice Fask's glance at Mackenzie, but she felt her heart race. Was this the point where she was going to be asked to speak? Kenth found her hand and squeezed it.

"No idea," Drayger admitted. "But the Compact ought to call one up, if not. Unless it's blown its load on the Alaskan monarchy, with all these excessive mates."

Mackenzie recognized that his crude humor was meant to hide how much the news had rattled him.

Tania touched his arm in a comforting fashion, and Toren, on his other side, murmured something that Mackenzie couldn't hear. Drayger brushed them both off.

"The Compact is in trouble," Fask said, and he gave a shorter and punchier explanation of what Mackenzie had told them in the Vault.

Mackenzie wasn't sure if she should feel offended that he hadn't let her make the big reveal or just relieved. She was coming to know everyone in the room, and trust them individually, but it still felt very alarming any time that they all looked at her at once.

They took the news with reactions that varied from amazement to disbelief.

"A person?" Raval said skeptically. "That's nonsense."

"Not a person, exactly," Fask corrected. "But something very complex and reactive."

Tania and Rian looked gravely at each other. "It's possible," she said. "It seems like a fanciful analogy, but… honestly, it does track."

Carina was delighted. "Why shouldn't the magical spell be sentient! But what's the problem if the Renewal fails? Why would more magic be a bad thing?"

Then everyone did turn and look at Mackenzie.

She swallowed. "It's not just that there's *more* magic, it's that magic doesn't have to follow rules anymore. Imagine having an argument with your neighbor and being able to crush their house with a careless thought, or starting a fire that will never go out. Magic takes intense focus to keep it from being immediate and subject to impulse. The Compact is like a grate in front of a fire, or a diffuser over a light that would blind you. It was a backstop—if there weren't enough parameters, the magic wouldn't work, so that there was a limit to what kind of chaos could happen. This…limitation would be gone without the Compact."

"Would *everyone* be able to do magic?" Raval asked in near horror.

Mackenzie could only shrug. "I don't know. I do know that Amara has been studying this for many years and that she has been trying to make *shortcuts* to magic. This probably looks like the greatest shortcut ever."

"Dalaya?" Kenth said quietly enough that only Mackenzie heard.

But he wasn't the only one who made that leap.

"Did she *shortcut* Dalaya?" Toren asked from down the table. "Is that why she can do what she can with drawings?"

Everyone was looking at Mackenzie again, and she shivered under their regard. The idea of Amara meddling with the little girl was absolutely horrifying, and it illustrated the danger of leaving magic wild. Summoning a fish and fixing her father was one thing, but what else might a tired and overwrought child with poor impulse control be capable of doing? "I don't honestly know," she said regretfully. "Amara had spells she wouldn't let me see, and I can't see the structure of magic once it's been cast."

"Can you imagine if everyone could do that?" Carina said, her voice sober. "Would it be *literally* everyone? Would we need to write anything down at all?"

"I know how dumb *I've* been at times," Toren told her, covering her hand with his. "Being able to do anything I imagined would be terrifying."

"It would certainly change the balance of power in a hurry," Fask said soberly.

"So all those times that Amara portaled here or sent her goons, she was after the Compact itself?"

They were looking at Mackenzie again.

"I don't know," she said, stuffing back her panic. "I think at first that she was just after anything magical, but when she realized how important and powerful the Compact was, she probably started making it more of a target."

"We still don't know how she's getting through wards," Raval said thoughtfully.

Mackenzie looked at him with sudden uncertainty, strong enough that Kenth glanced at her in concern. Did they not understand how portals worked?

Her suspicion was confirmed with Fask's shrug. "She must have something that neutralizes them."

"Wait, wait," Mackenzie said suddenly. "Those portal spells, they won't care about your wards, because they don't technically go through them. They have to be set from each end. Someone here had to place an anchor wherever they appeared on this side."

The entire table stared at her, and Mackenzie swallowed hard.

"Someone *here* had to set those up?" Raval repeated. "Someone *in* the castle?"

"Someone in my room at the hot springs?" Tania said in horror.

"In *my* room here?" Rian added.

Toren exclaimed, "Someone was in the *vault*?"

But Kenth's was the most alarming of all. "Someone was in *my daughter's bedroom*?"

"Are you sure?" Fask said, his voice icy. "Maybe you're wrong about that, too. You've said yourself that you can't see a spell once it's been cast."

"I-I saw those spells before they were used," Mackenzie said haltingly. Was she sure? She didn't feel very sure, under Fask's cool regard. Then she rallied herself. "Yes, I'm sure."

"It's kind of *odd* that you didn't bring that up before," Fask pointed out.

"I didn't think you...ah...didn't know," Mackenzie finished lamely. She didn't want to make them sound like idiots for not knowing something so basic.

Kenth was growling at Fask, undoubtedly picking up on Mackenzie's discomfort and laying the blame for it at his brother's door.

Captain Luke, just past Kenth, looked even more furious, in her totally self-contained, flinty-eyed way. "Then we have a traitor in the castle." She looked around the table and let her gaze linger on Drayger.

It wasn't missed.

Drayger spread his hands. "I've never been in the vault," he said. Then he winked at Tania. "Nor in your room, yet." He looked across at Kenth. "I don't even know where you've been the last few years!"

"Shadow might have left something in the vault," Carina pointed out. "Does it have an expiration date, or is it something that might have been left there, say, a few months ago?"

Mackenzie said, "The anchors are inert until they are activated by the spell itself."

"What would they look like?" Tania wanted to know.

"A small piece of paper, most likely, with the anchor spell written on it."

"A one-time use, then," Raval scoffed. "I still don't see the point of spending all that effort on a spell you can only use once."

"It's hard to get kids to carve things into stone?" Toren suggested wryly.

Fask pinched the bridge of his nose. "I don't want anyone leaving the castle. We have an entire army of new staff to keep tabs on, and all these *kids*." Mackenzie could hear the irritation in his voice.

"The staff is new," Rian pointed out. "We hadn't hired them when the portals were used against us."

"Does Amara have a lot more portal spells?" Raval wanted to know. "Can they use the previous anchors?"

Mackenzie couldn't answer those questions, or many of the others that followed, feeling more and more unhelpful until Fask impatiently called an end to the meeting so that the dining hall could be set for supper.

"We'll be tightening security," he promised. "No one is

to leave the immediate grounds. Luke, we'll coordinate an investigation of all current personnel, put a freeze on hiring. Keep guards on the kids, it's possible she'll try to take them back."

"I liked it better when Fask just did all this stuff himself," Raval complained as they were all rising to their feet and leaving.

"I think it's all a little more important now," Kenth said with resignation. His hand was in Mackenzie's, and it was as natural as breathing.

"Wait," Carina said, with sudden curiosity. "If the castle spirit is actually the Compact, what is Angel? Is she a spell, too?"

This drew everyone up for a thoughtful moment, but Mackenzie was completely lost. "Who is Angel?" she asked.

Kenth explained, "Angel is a…well, we thought she was a spirit in the same vein as our castle spirit. She controls the waters out at Angel Hot Springs."

"She likes to sit around in hot water making cryptic comments and playing pranks," Toren scoffed.

Carina giggled. "She raised the temperature of the water so that I passed out and Toren got all the fun of saving me from drowning."

"Like this," Toren demonstrated, sweeping her up into his arms. "I'll rescue you!"

He swept her out of the dining hall door as Carina slyly suggested in a stage whisper, "Your bed is probably really safe…"

Mackenzie glanced at Kenth to find that he was watching her with a smile lurking at the corners of his mouth. "My bed is probably really safe, too," he suggested. "And Mrs. James will be happy to keep an eye on Dalaya a little longer…"

CHAPTER 26

Whenever he could, Kenth avoided Fask in order to keep the peace, even knowing that his brother would assume it was because he was irresponsible and running away from his duties. He spent his days playing with Dalaya and falling even harder in love with Mackenzie.

The young woman was blooming in the light of the friendships that were offered to her. She won the hearts of everyone in the castle with her gentle strength and indomitable spirit. She caught up on modern media with Carina, talked books with Tania, and gravely asked for deportment advice from Leinani. Mrs. James already adored her for saving Kenth, and all the children worshiped her.

Even Fask seemed to set aside his suspicions of her, though Kenth suspected that there was more diplomacy than family fondness to his courtesy.

Dalaya took to her like a burr, insistent that only "Menzie" could play the right way, and talking non-stop about her whenever she wasn't there, hugging her as eagerly as Kenth himself at every chance she got.

Mackenzie herself seemed to soak it all up joyously and Kenth could feel her unfurling like a growing plant. She was curious and grateful for each opportunity to try something new and learn more of the things that seemed so commonplace to everyone else.

If she still carried darkness from her long time with the cult, sometimes waking from sleep with a gasp of fear, clutching her sweat-soaked covers to her, Kenth was not entirely free of his own demons, and he was happy to find that they could lean on each other unabashedly and trust each other completely.

He could comfort her when she shook with nerves or some piece of news rattled her memories of the cult. And she never hesitated to gentle him, when he was ready to rage at Fask's lack of action or his own mistakes.

Even without a mate bond at her end to give her clues to his moods, she always knew when he needed a distraction and was ready with a diversion, sometimes even exaggerating her own inabilities by pretending she needed help with her phone or the television.

They laughed together when he caught her doing that, and he felt like a better person for being with her.

"What are we going to do this afternoon?" she asked as they roused Dalaya together from a nap after lunch.

"Pull me in the sled!" Dalaya suggested.

Kenth glanced outside. It was a gray day, and it had snowed overnight; the trails probably weren't cleared yet. He wished he could take them out for a movie and a meal out, maybe show them the sights of Fairbanks, but Fask was adamant that it was too dangerous to leave the protection of the castle while so much was so uncertain.

Kenth didn't exactly disagree with him, for once.

CHAPTER 26

"Do you ever worry that you gave up one ivory tower for another?" he asked Mackenzie.

"I gave up a tower of *lies* for a place where I could actually *live*," she replied, and she tipped her head up and let him kiss her. "This is more freedom than I've ever had."

"Let's play a game," he suggested.

"Ol' May!" Dalaya said at once.

Kenth was heartily sick of Old Maid, but he played it stoically, hamming up his despair when he was stuck with the undesirable card at the end of the game. They played again until Dalaya got the Old Maid card and her despondency at losing made her pout and threaten tears.

Mackenzie tickled her back to laughter and took her on a tour of the castle that ended up with playing with the older kids. They were always delighted to take Dalaya and entertain her at a moment's notice. Very little progress had been made in reuniting them with their families, but the children didn't seem to mind. They had settled happily into life at the castle and showed little interest in looking over the cold case missing children reports to try to identify themselves.

"Amara made a big point of saying that their parents didn't want them," Mackenzie told Kenth privately. "I don't know how much of that was lies, to secure her hold over them, and how much of it was truth. She would probably go for easy pickings, orphans, kids in foster care, children that wouldn't be missed, reported, or pursued."

"Then she must have wanted Dalaya in particularly for something," Kenth mused. "She had to know that I wouldn't rest until I got her back."

They exchanged a long, thoughtful look. Dalaya had not manifested any magic since she'd saved Kenth's life. Kenth only let her draw when Mackenzie was on hand to watch her and warn her away if she felt anything that resembled casting, but so far she had not been interested in doing more than drawing puppies and sleds and cupcakes.

Only *pictures* of puppies and sleds and cupcakes.

"She'll be busy with the kids for a while," Kenth said suggestively. "What would you like to do next for Plan Fun?"

Mackenzie's face glowed. "Something…grown up?"

"I know just the thing," Kenth said merrily.

~

"What is it?" he asked that night, after they had tucked Dalaya into her bed together for a third time and it looked likely to stick. He could feel that something was bothering Mackenzie, and he thought he could see it in her clouded expression, but there wasn't enough finesse in the bond to tell him *what*.

She didn't dissemble or pretend that he couldn't read her, magic or not. "Will you tell me about her mother when you're ready?" she asked hesitantly, and Kenth wondered how much of her reluctance he could read from her face and her voice and how much he got from their bond.

Secrets. So many layers of secrets.

Would he ever truly be ready to share them?

She deserved all the truths, Kenth thought. All the ugly realities, along with all of the treasured memories.

They walked from Dalaya's room into his sitting room, and when they might have otherwise retreated for his bedroom, he led her instead to the big plush couch that looked out over the forest that stretched away from the castle out into the wilderness.

They hadn't turned on the lights in the room; it was dark enough inside that they could see outside the windows instead of only a reflection, where the faint illumination from the moon outside etched the snow-covered hills and trees in silver.

"You don't have to," she assured him. "Dalaya says she makes you sad."

"I want to tell you," Kenth said solemnly, sitting and drawing her down beside him in the dark. "These are things you should know."

She snuggled into his side, and Kenth could feel her selflessly willing strength and support and affection into him, knowing that he would pick it up. Was it reading too much into a feeling like that to think that it was love? It wasn't just that she was sharing his bed; she was definitely fond of him, and even though the mate bond was starting to fade, Kenth was still certain that she *could* love him. *Might* love him.

Did love him?

What did he even know about love?

"I know she died in a snowmobile crash," Mackenzie said. "I know that Fask knew about her. I know that no one talks about it."

"Snowmachine," Kenth said automatically. "We call it a snowmachine."

Mackenzie was quiet, and Kenth scrubbed at his face, recognizing that he'd only *corrected* her because he didn't want to *answer* her.

"We don't have to—"

"It's not a long story and I should tell it to you. I was Dana's rebound," he said gruffly. "She loved Fask, and he hurt her, and later she settled for me and I always wanted to be enough for her and never was."

Mackenzie sat up so that she could look at him, her eyes barely visible in the dark. "You don't *know* that," she said confidently. "I don't believe it for a moment."

"I know that I wasn't enough to keep her from being reckless and getting herself killed. She went out in bad conditions, alone, and got caught in an avalanche." Shouldn't he have been able to protect her?

"Is Dalaya...?" Mackenzie trailed off reluctantly, probably trying to string together a timeline.

"Dalaya is mine," Kenth clarified. "There isn't any doubt."

"This explains a lot about you and Fask," Mackenzie said quietly.

"This is the least of our problems," Kenth said. He realized how sour he sounded and made an effort to soften his voice. "Fask blames me for our mother's death. I'm not sure he's wrong."

"That wasn't your fault, either," Mackenzie said firmly.

"I was supposed to be somewhere, and I wasn't. But...Mom was. There was a flash flood, it was breakup, all the ice of the river was going out, and she got swept out in it. If I'd been there, where I was *supposed* to be, I could have saved her."

"You couldn't have known there would be a flood," Mackenzie pointed out.

"But if I'd *been* there..." Kenth said achingly. He remembered flying over the broken river, searching the ice in vain for his mother.

Mackenzie curled closer to his side and he could feel the comfort and trust in her, like she was trying to will it to him.

"I failed both of them," Kenth said mournfully.

"Don't you think Dana loved Dalaya?"

"Of course she loved her daughter. What does that have to do with anything?" Kenth tried to gentle his words, but he only wanted to shove it all away, deny it, ignore it, and he knew that his anger was clear in his voice.

Mackenzie's voice was carefully measured and she found Kenth's hand in the darkness. "If Dalaya couldn't keep her from being reckless, why would you think that it was proof she didn't love you, that you couldn't keep her safe? She was careless and unlucky and you loved her, and you are still angry with her for leaving you alone to take care of Dalaya because you don't feel equal to it."

"I am so angry," Kenth admitted. "I am so angry and tired and I want things to be simple and straight-forward and they never are. Dammit."

Mackenzie laughed lightly and took his hand into hers. "You're a great dad," she assured him. "Nothing worth doing is ever easy."

But somehow, this *was*.

Loving Mackenzie, whatever complications came along with that, was far and away the easiest thing he'd ever done.

She was his other half, his perfect mate. She thought she was flawed, and Kenth could feel her wistful regret that she couldn't experience the mate bond like he did, but he didn't care a bit for that, or for any of the things that she worried might make her unfit for him.

They were both perfectly broken in ways that fit together like clockwork, and when he leaned to kiss her, everything about her softened in welcome.

"Mackenzie." He took the side of her face in one hand —in part to simplify finding her mouth in the darkness and in part because he loved the feel of her cheek against his palm so dearly. "Mackenzie, you don't have to ever worry about comparing yourself to Dana, about wondering if I think of her when I hold you. I loved her then and I love you now, with my whole heart. I never confuse what I felt for her with what I feel now, and I don't need the future flashes of the mate bond to remind me to hold on to you."

He stroked her cheek with a tender thumb. "I wouldn't have recognized you without the mate bond, but I don't need it to know you now, and I don't need magic to tell me how perfect you are for me. I love you, Mackenzie."

He felt the unspoken tension in her chest suddenly give like a snapping harp string, and there was a rush of love that felt *now* in her heart.

She didn't say it back, but she did kiss him, and there weren't many words after that at all.

CHAPTER 27

Fask was closing the door to the vault when Kenth came down the steps.

"You're going to see Father," Fask said. It wasn't a question.

At another time, Kenth wouldn't have slowed his steps or alter his path, not wanting to give Fask the satisfaction of making him move to the far side of the hallway or pausing politely. But he realized to his surprise that he didn't want to quarrel with his brother. He shrugged. "Yes."

"He's not really there, you know," Fask said. "He's not going to have any answers for you."

"I didn't ask *you,*" Kenth growled out of habit, walking past Fask.

"Maybe you *should* ask me," Fask pointed out acidly, and Kenth came to a stop but didn't turn. Fask was clearly spoiling for a fight. "Maybe *I've* been here the whole time doing all the work while you were off sulking in the wilderness. Maybe *I'm* the one who actually sees what's going on. You just come back and think you can bull your way to the top without even stopping to look at everything that got done—that *I* got done—while you were gone."

Kenth turned back. "I don't want to be king, Fask. You can keep the crown. I didn't ask for any of this."

Frustration seethed off of Fask. "Then why are you questioning every damned thing I do or say, in front of everyone else? Leading people off on daring, *stupid* escapades when a little caution is prudent? You've all but led a mutiny of our brothers. If you don't want to be king, you're sure doing a great job of making it clear you don't want *me* to be king."

Kenth gritted his teeth. "I've never said that." Why was this coming up *now*?

"You didn't have to. You just make it obvious that you don't respect me or any of the choices I have to make. You abandoned your family, you abandoned me, just as everything here was going to hell. Now you want to come back and be a goddamn hero and you're not. You're not the good guy here."

Kenth felt the sting of Fask's words like a wolf pack biting at his heels. Was he being unreasonable? Was he in the wrong, to flaunt Fask's authority, when he'd never desired it himself?

He steeled himself. If he'd done as Fask said and obediently waited, they never would have rescued Dalaya or the other children.

Fask wasn't always right.

And Kenth wasn't always wrong.

"You do what you need to, brother," he said tightly. "If you want to save face, don't try to tighten my leash or tell me how to raise *my* daughter."

Fask met his gaze with distrust and dislike, like always. "I'm not trying to *control* you," he said through gritted teeth. "You *or* Mackenzie. I just don't want to have to clean up after you again."

Kenth opened his mouth to hurl back an automatic protest or an insult, and then closed it again. He didn't want to fight with Fask. He recognized now that his brother's blame was based in grief, and that his anger was steeped in regret. The past was past, and Kenth would not change a single moment of his pain if it meant not having Dalaya, or not having Mackenzie.

While he was chewing over this revelation, Fask took his hesitation as a triumph. "Turn off the lights when you leave," he said in his irritating voice of superiority. "There's no reason to waste electricity." Then he was stalking off down the hallway towards the stairs up to the castle.

Kenth prowled in the other direction, deeper into the earth, until he came to the door at the end.

The door to their father's resting place was the same size and style as the vault door, and it opened with the same magic, part of the same, far-reaching spell that would be refreshed with the Renewal. "*Baliankenth.*"

It swung open soundlessly, on perfectly balanced hinges, but the lighting was completely mundane; Kenth flipped up a light switch by the door and gentle overhead spotlights came on.

This was the original vault site of the Alaskan dragons, outgrown several generations ago. Kenth remembered, distantly, hauling their father's sleeping form down the tunnel to this place when the slumbering dragon shape had proved increasingly inconvenient for keeping secrets in the castle above.

So many secrets.

Moving him here had been Fask's idea, and Kenth had fought it tooth and nail, but his brothers had outvoted him, and his strength had been required for the move. He remembered growling and grumbling as they slung the dead weight of their father down the wide stairs and down the dark hallway.

Dead weight.

Kenth hoped that the term was not prophetic.

Part of his anger had been mixed up with grief and fear. He didn't want to rule. He didn't want Fask to rule. He wanted their father, grave and wise, and with them again.

He didn't fill the room the way Kenth remembered. Had he shrunk in size as well as power over the intervening years? For a grim moment, Kenth thought he was truly dead; there was no breath from the massive dragon, no steady heartbeat. The room was silent and tomb-like, despite the cheerful light.

Then there was a slow, measured thrum.

And after a few minutes, another.

His great heart still beat. Somewhere, under those scales, in that broad chest, his heart still worked.

Did he still love? Did he still mourn their mother?

There was a breath, from the still form, so slow that it barely stirred Kenth's hair as he approached. Then an inhale, as slow and imperceptible.

"Father," Kenth said into the terrible quiet. "Father, I'm back, for now."

He wasn't sure what else to say. What had Mackenzie said, bearing witness to his own coma? He hadn't really heard her, only felt the poison-distant swirl of her emotions through their one-sided mate bond.

There was a chair off to the side and Kenth drew it up closer to his father's slumbering head and sat back in it. Did Raval come down here? Fask wouldn't. Raval had been closer with their mother than their father, though.

CHAPTER 27

Maybe one of the younger brothers? Tray certainly wouldn't. Rian wasn't that sentimental. Toren...Toren had grown up a shocking amount in the past five years and Kenth could imagine him coming down here to ask advice when faced with the prospect of suddenly being king.

A prospect that was only infinitely more complicated now that there was a fourth mate in the mix.

"I have a little girl now," he thought to tell the silent dragon. "Her name is Dalaya, she's a feisty five years old, and you'd love her. She'd love you, too." It was hard to think about his stately father as a doting grandfather. "She'd probably climb all over you, given the chance. She's fearless and smart and she's got the whole castle wrapped around her little finger."

Except for Fask, who still looked at her with mistrust... and maybe regret.

"I have a mate now, too," Kenth went on. "Just as smart and fearless. She's beautiful and brave and we...suit each other really well." It seemed like a gross understatement. How was he supposed to unpack the adventures that they'd had and the way he felt every time that he saw her or sensed her presence? How did you sum up 'my everythings' into a few shabby descriptions? His father wouldn't care if Mackenzie was a castaway from a cult or if Dalaya could do magic, or any of the complicated dramas that made succession a puzzle now.

He'd care that Mackenzie was smiling more now than ever, and that Dalaya was learning to tie her shoes.

He'd care...he'd care if Kenth was *happy*.

And Kenth was stunned to realize that he was.

However the thrones and the Renewal worked out, whether Fask ruled or any of his brothers did, Kenth had a daughter he adored and a mate that completed him. His life held a note of optimism that overshadowed all the uncertainty. He had *family*.

He hadn't realized how much he longed for it, hidden away on his own. He had missed his brothers. Even Fask, for all of his smugness and self-righteousness and Kenth's simmering desire to hit him into next week.

"I...I wish I could ask you what it was like, with mother, with us when we were young. What it would be like being king. I'd like to ask whether I should be the king or let Fask have that thankless task. He wants it, I don't. I didn't ask for any of this. Did you? I don't remember you as anything but a king. Who were you before that? How did you learn to be confident? How do I remain as patient as you always were?"

Now that he was asking questions, they flooded out of him. "Why would the Compact tap four of us? What does it mean for the Renewal? Which I guess is more important than we ever realized. Dad, I could really use your advice right now."

The dragon was silent in reply, a slow beat of his heart the only answer.

Kenth let his breath out in a tired sigh. "Thanks for the pep talk, Dad," he said ironically as he got to his feet.

He flipped the light switch off on his way out, not keen to get a lecture from Mrs. James about wasting electricity, and told himself that it wasn't because Fask had told him to.

CHAPTER 28

"What do you want most in the world?" Kenth asked.

They were lying together in his huge bed, enjoying a moment of peace late in the morning before Dalaya woke up.

Mackenzie considered, looking up at the carved wooden ceiling of the spacious room. She was on a heavenly bed covered in sheets of a thread-count she'd never even known was possible, reclined on down pillows, and there was a handsome prince lying beside her tracing lazy patterns on her skin with worship in his eyes.

She thought about all the things she'd read about and longed for as a girl: true love, adventure, riches, power...

"I want to fly," she said softly. "I want to be free in the sky, with the world small below me."

She realized too late that Kenth had probably been offering a gift, not a fantasy. She should have picked something he could *buy* her. He must think she was being too unrealistic and childish.

"I could take you up on my back," Kenth said thoughtfully, but Mackenzie thought that they both knew that it wouldn't be what she was really asking for. "It's not really much more comfortable than being carried, though. It would be windy, cold, and dangerous. It's not as glamorous as you might think."

She wished she could feel him through the mate bond, to really know what he was thinking. She imagined that she could sense him sometimes, but it was undoubtedly only what she read in his face or guessed from his voice.

He must have sensed her stab of insecurity, because he rolled over and wrapped her in his arms. "I know a better way to fly," he said suggestively, and when his mouth covered hers, Mackenzie forgot to worry about how he might have taken her foolish wish.

It was only, for the moment, the two of them, limbs sliding over smooth bedding as he stroked her with a finger for the few moments it took for her to become slick and ready. He was hard again, and they were unhurried and exploring all the ways to be with each other that felt so right.

If she wished, desperately, that she could feel him in her head as she fell from the heights of pleasure that he coaxed her to, it didn't diminish her enjoyment in the slightest.

And it *was* a little like flying, like having outspread wings held up by air currents, gliding down from sweet release.

~

It was a little like flying later, too, racing down the Big Slope in a sled with Dalaya and Kenth. He'd brought his own sled this time, and half a dozen of the older kids, so they were taking turns climbing breathlessly to the top and gliding down to crash in the giant fluffy snowbanks at the bottom. Even their ubiquitous guards were enjoying themselves and taking turns sledding down with the children.

The air was full of laughter and ease, and Mackenzie thought she had never been as happy and carefree.

She felt safe here, protected and loved.

It wasn't just Kenth, though so much of it was. It was also Dalaya, who trusted her and gave her hugs and kisses without strings. It was Kenth's brothers—even, at last, Fask—and their mates, and the way they had opened their home to her. They liked her, she thought, and her love-starved heart felt full at last, overflowing like she'd never known was possible.

She and Dalaya shrieked together down the slide, toppling together at the last moment into one of the snowbanks and rolling in happy laughter as they collected the sled and got out of the way of the next one that was flying down the hill full of screaming children.

"Menzie? Menzie?"

Mackenzie had been looking up the hill to where Kenth was preparing to push Cindy and Elijah down in their own sled. He waved enthusiastically and Mackenzie waved back.

"Menzie," Dalaya said more urgently, tugging at Mackenzie's coat. "I have to go potty."

"Whoops," Mackenzie said, turning back to her. "Well, we'd better head back to the castle, darling. Want me to pull you?"

"Pull me fast!" Dalaya said, climbing eagerly into the sled and nearly falling over as Mackenzie took off. One of the guards fell into step behind them, but this didn't bother Mackenzie; guards had shadowed her all of her life.

Mackenzie turned and waved back up the slope at the

curve that took them across the lake and back to the castle. The very small and distant form of Kenth waved back and Mackenzie hurried on to the castle.

They got to the bathroom just in time, Dalaya shedding her coat and boots and snow pants along the way, their guard taking up his place just outside the door to the suite.

"Feel better?" Mackenzie asked kindly as the little girl finished washing her hands and emerged from the bathroom. She had collected all of Dalaya's winter gear and was shaking the snow off of it. It sounded like someone had started a fire in Kenth's sitting room. "Want a cup of hot chocolate in front of the fire?" she offered.

Dalaya stared through the open door with big eyes. "Menzie?" she said, and her voice had a thin thread of terror that made Dalaya realize she wasn't hearing a fire at all.

Amara herself stood in front of the brilliant portal.

"I won't go back with you," Mackenzie said, drawing to her feet with her teeth bared. Her heart froze in her chest, the shock of seeing Amara again so unexpected that it was like she'd been struck in the head. "Dalaya, stay behind me."

Dalaya, for once, was instantly obedient. Mackenzie wasn't sure if it was because she'd accepted Mackenzie as an authority figure, or if it was because she remembered Amara and rightly feared her.

"I'm not here for you," Amara said gently. It was her reasonable voice, the one she used to say the most terrible things. "I'm here for the one who *wasn't* a failure. I heard about the goldfish, dear Dalaya."

"No." Mackenzie felt Dalaya press up behind her, wrapping her arms around Mackenzie's knees. She steeled herself. "I won't let you take her. Your magic won't work on me,. You can't make me give her up."

"I don't need my magic to work on you," Amara said, and a little of her mask of manners slipped. "I can control you without it."

Mackenzie scowled at her. "You think you have all the answers and you never did," she said fiercely. "I don't follow you anymore. You can't force me to agree with you, and you can't force me to help you."

"Oh, but I can," Amara said, her voice silky and sure as she looked beyond Mackenzie and Dalaya at the sound of a commotion.

Mackenzie turned, keeping Dalaya behind her, to assess this new threat, and felt her heart drop to her stomach. If she'd had a working mate bond, she would already have known who was behind her. It was Kenth, his face showing snarling rage as he was held between two of Amara's guards. Mackenzie wondered for a split second why he didn't simply shift and break free of them, then recognized the carved bead-and-leather choker at his throat.

A control necklace like the ones Amara had used on Tray and Leinani, specifically designed to keep a dragon from shifting.

Kenth must have come for Mackenzie when he felt her panic at seeing Amara, and been caught in a trap.

If they'd come to the castle together, she could have seen the spell before it activated and stopped it. Mackenzie was appalled to realize that someone here, in the castle, must have recognized this opportunity and laid the trap and set the anchor for the portal in the short time that she was helping Dalaya.

"I'm sure you know how the necklace works," Amara said. "You will all come with me, now, quietly."

Dalaya made a muffled noise of alarm.

"Leave them alone!" Mackenzie said, exactly as Kenth said in horror, "Don't hurt them!"

"It's so charming how you all pretend to care. Did he tell you that he was your mate?" Amara asked. "It's just lies, you know. They are trying to manipulate you, to use you against me. You want to believe the best of them because your head has been filled with pretty stories and promises, but you are not a princess and he does *not* love you."

Kenth made a wordless growl of protest and Mackenzie actually laughed out loud.

"If you had wanted to prove to me that you did not understand love, you could not have done it better," she said, feeling strangely detached. She wasn't angry with Amara, she didn't hate the woman who had controlled her and lied to her all of her life.

She only pitied her.

She pitied Amara's hollow power and her fear and her grasping for relevance.

"You think love is about power, about control, and it never was. Love is not the size of a heart, but the size of a soul. I won't let you take Dalaya again," Mackenzie said firmly. "And if you try to hurt Kenth, I *will* fight you," Mackenzie warned. "I won't let you take his dragon."

"I won't have to hurt either of them if you come with me quietly," Amara said dismissively. "He is merely my assurance of his daughter's cooperation, and yours."

"You can't have them," Kenth growled, earning himself a cuff at the side of the head from one of Amara's guard's beside him.

There was pounding on the door. The castle guard?

Mackenzie saw the moment that Amara put the glamor into motion. Dalaya went slack and blinked several times. Kenth shook his head and stopped resisting his guards. The glazed look in his eyes was the most heart-stopping thing that Mackenzie had ever seen in her life. His gaze went right past her to caress Amara with enchanted devotion.

Amara could take him from her this way, steal his will, and Mackenzie had never seen anything so terrible.

"I can't use magic on you, you malfunctioning ingrate," Amara said coldly. "But I can use magic on him and you know that I will."

"Don't hurt him," Mackenzie repeated, feeling cornered and defeated. "I'll come with you. I'll serve at your side again. Just don't hurt him. Leave him here with his daughter. Leave them alone forever." It was better never to see him again than to see him like *this*.

One of Amara's guards bound Kenth's hands—he offered them eagerly to be tied, proof of his idolatry. Dalaya looked up at him with vacant obedience.

"The Hand?" the guard asked.

"Bring her," Amara said. "Having a pair was unexpectedly useful with his brother."

To her surprise, Mackenzie recognized the destination of the portal. "America?" she said, looking around as they walked through. "The state of Oregon."

"I'm amazed that you remember it," Amara said, stepping through. "You were very young when we were last living here."

They were her earliest memories, and they weren't particularly happy. Mackenzie let her guards prod her through the portal to the shabby lodge. The other side was outdoors, on a wide deck overlooking a canyon filled with snowy trees. It was easier to look around and remember playing near the dangerous dropoff than it was to look at Kenth and see him adoring Amara.

So she was caught completely by surprise when he suddenly barreled sideways into the guard holding Dalaya's hand, giving a war cry. He twisted down to pick his daughter up with his bound hands and toss her backward through the portal towards the couch, shouting "Alto!" as she cleared the magical threshold. Dalaya gave a cry of shock and dismay that cut off abruptly as the portal closed with a crackle.

"No! How did he break free?" Amara said in outrage. "Stop him!"

Her guards were still completely enchanted, and even if they hadn't been her most loyal followers, they would have done as she said. One of them lowered his weapon and Mackenzie saw what it might do and gave a scream of horror a split second before it fired.

There was a blast of sizzling purple magic and Kenth fell to the ground.

"You fool!" Amara raged. "He was our assurance of her cooperation, and a dragon that we might have used, and you *killed* him!"

Mackenzie's breath caught in her throat, turning from air into salt.

Killed him? Kenth was dead?

He lay still at the guards' feet, and as hard as Mackenzie willed him to stand, to move, to breath, to do *anything*, he didn't stir at all.

Amara nudged him with a foot and his arm fell away from his side limply. "Not even a dragon would survive that," she said in disgust. "You fools have failed me and she is useless to me now."

CHAPTER 29

It was a moment or two before Kenth regained consciousness, his dragon all but dragging him back to awareness, and he was careful to stay still.

We've been together through worse than that, his dragon scoffed. And while that was true, it wasn't entirely comfortable. Was life *now* worth those three days screaming in pain? Kenth wasn't entirely sure yet because he still wasn't entirely sure that he was *alive*.

"Wait, before you kill me, who *was* my mother?" Mackenzie was demanding. "What did you do to her? What did you do to *me*?"

It wasn't timid Mackenzie's voice; it was Mackenzie-who-knew-herself who spoke, and Kenth had a surge of pride for her. Whatever happened next, Mackenzie had grown into all of her potential and possibilities, and he was so glad to have had some part in that journey.

He also really hoped that this wasn't the end of the journey for either of them.

Mackenzie thought it was, he realized through their mate bond. She thought he was dead and all of his efforts to *think really loud* at her failed. His assurances only echoed back to himself. He could not tell her that he was okay without tipping off to their captors that he was still a threat, and he knew that his only chance of winning this uneven battle was to somehow use surprise to his advantage.

Don't do anything foolish, he wished he could remind her, because he could feel her desperation and despair. She was resolved to stop Amara at any cost, because she was sure that she had already paid the ultimate price. She was just hoping to get information out of Amara before she ended her forever.

Careful, Kenth wanted to warn her. Amara was savvy, and she wouldn't trust Mackenzie anymore.

"I was your mother, of course," Amara said, in a tone that sounded entirely too reasonable.

"You weren't," Mackenzie said flatly. "You're mixing up your own lies."

"I was your mother in every way that mattered," Amara said. "I raised you after your traitor mother rejected the Cause."

"What did you try to do to Dalaya?" Mackenzie asked, and Kenth's heart skipped a beat. Dalaya. As if he didn't have enough reasons already to shake off the pounding pain in his head and help Mackenzie defeat the madwoman. Was his daughter safe on the other side of the portal?

"I thought it didn't work," Amara said with a smirk. "But apparently, it turned out even more impressively than I had hoped. I heard about the fish sandwich. The spell didn't work on *you* because your birth mother stopped me, but there was no one to stop me from making Dalaya what I needed her to be. All I needed was dragon blood, and a spell to unlock all your potential and release you from the *rules*."

"My mother was a dragon?" Kenth could feel Mackenzie's astonishment behind her rage.

"No, your mother was a caster," Amara said scornfully. "Your father was a dragon."

"What happened to my mother?" Mackenzie asked calmly. Kenth was alarmed by the desperation behind her even voice. "Who were my parents?"

"I'm done with your questions," Amara said. "Throw her off the cliff. She's of no use to me now."

This was Kenth's moment, he thought. Even with his arms bound, he could overpower the guards if he surprised them. If he could get to his feet quickly enough, maybe he could slam them into the wall. They looked almost as large as he was, but surely they didn't have dragon-fast reflexes or strength. If he could neutralize them, he could give Mackenzie a chance to take Amara out herself.

Mackenzie was angry enough now, her grief crystallized into fury, and Kenth thought he was braced for anything she might do, ready to back her up however he could.

But he was not in the slightest bit prepared for what happened next.

CHAPTER 30

*K*enth was dead.

Mackenzie's heart was like a block of ice in her chest. If she let it thaw for even a moment, she knew she would break down uselessly, so she kept it cold and distant and didn't look at Kenth's still body or let herself think about him.

She had only one purpose left. To stop Amara, forever, and make sure that she couldn't make anyone else suffer.

And she had no idea how to do that. Amara had shields and guards and Mackenzie was unarmed. They had spells that—even if they wouldn't work *on* Mackenzie, they would work around her. She would never be trusted again, to get close to Amara and slip a blade between her ribs. Mackenzie was both shocked to think of the idea and angry with herself that it still gave her pause.

She couldn't pause. She couldn't hesitate. She had to keep her purpose.

So she asked questions. All the questions she had always wanted answers to. Who was she? Where did she come from? Why was she like she was? None of Amara's replies were satisfying.

Mackenzie closed her eyes, looking for the answers inside of her.

There had to be a reason for the silence in her soul, her mute refusal of all magic. It was as if something had been sealed off from her, as if she was missing something... something that belonged to her. Her mother...had protected her from the spell that had made Dalaya a chaotic caster.

She thought it was only her memories, perhaps blocked off to protect her from some trauma she'd suffered as a child. But now, listening with every fiber of her being, she felt that it was more like something had been walled away from her deliberately. There was something there behind the barrier that wasn't just her own mind.

Something beating to be free.

Some*one*.

She let herself think about Kenth for the first time since he had fallen, overwhelmed with grief and pain. He had taught her to love, not only him, but herself, and he had shown her all the light and joy that the world had to offer.

Without him, she was in darkness again.

And when the light went out, she could see through the glass in her soul.

It wasn't just a hazy, warped reflection of herself, in this quiet place inside of her. It was her other half.

It was her *dragon*.

This was what Amara had tried so desperately to keep from her, shrouding her in secrets and misinformation.

There was a dragon in her soul, trapped, like the rest of her, in a bubble that repelled all magic.

Now that she knew what she was looking at, Mackenzie

could see the spell that had countered every other spell that touched her. Her mother's last, fiery, fatal act had been to protect her, and in doing so, she had caged the part of her that Amara had originally been after: her *dragon*.

The side effect of making her immune to magic was accidental, she thought, as she brushed the tendrils and swirls of the spell with her mind. Love. Devotion. Fear. Loyalty. Compassion. The spell had kept her buoyed through times of hardship and terror when she hadn't even recognized it.

It was starting to fade, because all spells faded, even spells as complex as the Compact. Those faint, fleeting moments that she thought she felt the mate bond had been leaks around the boundaries of the decaying spell. It was fraying at the edges.

And she didn't need it anymore.

Mackenzie breathed deep, remembered Kenth teaching her what happiness was, and ripped away the magic shielding her heart—and her dragon—at last.

It hurt.

Like a bandage that took skin with it, she tore it from within her and cast it away, and the dragon who had been buried inside her came alive and awake, roaring out of her in protest of her long, lonely imprisonment.

Free! Free! Free!

Her body changed, breaking apart and re-building itself in a rush of power as she spread wings and grew claws and felt her jaw stretch into a long, fierce snout. Scales rippled over her, and horns stretched from her head as she arched her neck and snarled.

Amara and the guard holding her by the shoulder were tossed aside by the transformation. Mackenzie was still trying to make sense of her new limbs and appendages as the cult leader scrambled to her feet and tried to run.

Mackenzie stopped her with a jolt of flame directly in her path and nearly choked on the smoky aftermath. Flaming had been instinctive, but she realized it was like swallowing and breathing—it could be done wrong if you weren't used to it. She coughed, shook her head, then advanced. She could tear Amara to pieces with her claws and teeth if she had to; fire wasn't her only weapon.

That was the moment that she realized that Kenth still lived.

She had barely noticed in the storm of her dragon's return, but she could feel the mate bond now, and she knew the truth and power of his undeniable love for her. It wasn't just her memory of that love, he was there in her mind, and he was *alive*.

Even as she grappled with the relief and joy of this discovery, he used the chaos of her transformation to surge to his feet to surprise the guards that were starting to raise weapons against her.

Mackenzie froze a moment, divided between the guards who battled with Kenth and Amara herself.

"Mackenzie!" Amara tried to protest. "You can't kill me! I was like a mother to you!"

But Mackenzie knew what a parent's love was like now, had witnessed what family could be, and she opened her mouth to snap Amara up just as the woman shrieked, "Throw him over!"

It was the only thing that might have stopped her, and Mackenzie's head swiveled to witness Amara's goons heaving Kenth's struggling form off the bluff.

Without thinking about it, Mackenzie turned from Amara, charged two steps, and flung herself from the bluff to catch his falling body.

The only problem was that she didn't know how to fly.

CHAPTER 31

She was a dragon.

Kenth's brain was muddled and his ears were still ringing from the aftermath of whatever they'd shot him with, but he didn't for a moment doubt his eyes.

Mackenzie was *a dragon.*

It made so much sense and explained so much: her resistance to the cold, her indomitable spirit, her mysterious past. Amara had tried to steal her power and only trapped it inside of her.

And Mackenzie was the most gorgeous dragon he'd ever seen, her hide a dark iridescent rainbow of colors, her neck snaking gracefully as she advanced on Amara.

Then Kenth was too busy trying to avoid being thrown off a cliff to admire her, and failing, because the hateful necklace kept him from shifting and his arms were tied. He was shifter-strong and shifter-fast, but they overpowered him easily.

The dragon that was Mackenzie followed him over, but she tumbled and fell. Kenth knew from experience that she'd snapped her wings out too fast and probably strained them as she jumped after him. She didn't know immediately how to fold them down to dive, so she wasted valuable falling time tangled with them and fighting the air drag.

Kenth watched her and despaired, hoping only that she would figure out flight before she hit the bottom of the ravine, and that she wouldn't feel his own graceless, fatal landing.

She seemed to straighten, her wings flat against her back, and then closed the gap between them with furious determination. Kenth closed his eyes, knowing that they must be too close to the ground for her to save him now and that her steep, uncontrolled dive could only break her neck. *Let me go,* he begged. *Save yourself!* It would be more convenient if dragons could speak mind to mind, but he knew his words were only echoing in his own head, and he knew Mackenzie would do anything to save him.

Did he imagine that the mate bond in his head was somehow stronger?

He felt like she was warmer, somehow, that her emotions were clearer. That fondness that had bloomed into deep love was singing now, and it felt as if it was wrapping him...wrapping him in gentle strands of glowing power.

Impossibly, he was slowing in his downward plunge, as if he was being caught in invisible rope, and when Mackenzie spread her wings and struggled to slow her descent, he was yanked with her, despite the distance between them.

Her flight was erratic and desperate, her wings beating awkwardly as she turned her fall into upward force, and Kenth realized how close to the ground they had come when he crashed sideways into the top of a tree. Needles dragged along his skin and branches snapped.

Mackenzie strained her wings harder, just able to pull him over the next tree, but not the next. The top of it broke off from his impact. Mackenzie dropped a few dozen feet, taking Kenth's stomach with her, and he was in freefall for a terrible moment before he was caught again as she flapped higher and found herself fighting the treetops.

She quickly gave up on flying away with him and settled for getting him safely to the ground, battling through forest cover to lower him to the snowy ground before collapsing herself. The invisible bonds of power that had caught Kenth seemed to dissolve.

Kenth had to wrestle himself upright out of a snowbank, his arms still tied, and turned his snowy face to where Mackenzie was trying to fold her wings; they were at impossible angles and caught in branches all around her. She started to turn, keened as one of her trapped wings dragged her back, and then shifted into human form, falling to her knees in snow.

"Mackenzie!" Kenth was up on his feet and charging for her, but he couldn't embrace her with his arms restrained, and his attempt only landed him on his face in the snow. "Mackenzie!" he sputtered.

She picked him up and put her arms around him, and they stood there a long moment, Mackenzie trembling and crying. "Oh, Kenth. I thought I'd lost you."

"You saved me," he murmured into her hair.

"I love you," she said. "I know you already knew, but I know now, too. I love you, I *love* you." She kissed him desperately and Kenth struggled against his bonds trying to embrace her and only tipped them both over again into a snowbank.

She sniffed and wiped her face as she pulled him back to a seated position.

"I can't make love to you all tied up like this," Kenth protested.

"You *could,*" she purred. "And we should try it some time, but maybe not in these conditions."

Kenth's imagination supplied the conditions that would work much better and Mackenzie blushed through her tears. "I *felt* that," she said, giggling in embarrassment and delight. "You *like* the idea."

"So do you," Kenth pointed out. "You *really* like the idea. You have a surprisingly dirty mind, don't you!"

"I blame the librarians," Mackenzie said. "You would not believe the books they recommend."

Kenth turned so that she could work at the knots on his wrists behind him. "I would like to read those books," he decided.

He felt her sober in his head as she fought with his bonds and looked up the cliff they'd just careened down. "Amara is getting away," she said regretfully, picking at the knots with increasing frustration. "These might have been easier to untie if you hadn't struggled so much."

"Forget about Amara. We'll bring her to justice later. She didn't get Dalaya. She didn't get you."

"Ah!" Mackenzie cried in triumph as she finally got the last knot untied. "You're free!"

Kenth rolled his sore shoulders and made the mistake of touching the necklace binding him to human form. Mackenzie hissed with his pain. "Almost free," she corrected herself.

"Sorry," he said. "There are downsides to feeling the bond."

"There are more upsides," she said, caressing his cheek and smiling at him in wonder. "I'm sorry I missed so much of it. Is it already a lot weaker now?"

Kenth considered, drawing Mackenzie into his arms

the way he'd been dying to. He could still feel all the waves of her emotions and desire, and the fading pain in her side, and the strength of her spirit, but it was all less noisy now, less full of echoes. "I still feel you," he said thoughtfully. "But we're closer now to our true possibility, so there's less *chatter*, if that makes sense."

"It does," Mackenzie said, her voice and her heart full of contentment. "It's not just that I *might* love you or may trust you, but that I *do.*" She was touching him like she couldn't resist it, and Kenth knew that she was getting a head full of the desire that she raised in him with every stroke and caress.

He kissed her and drank in the reflections of his own desire, like they were feeding each other with their own pleasure. "Mackenzie, my love," he murmured near her ear, and that was the best of all, because he knew that she could feel it and not fail to believe it. He accidentally brushed his necklace trying to get her hair back and they shivered apart. "I don't suppose that you can get this off of me?"

Mackenzie concentrated, and Kenth felt her surprise and regret. "The others could only be removed by the one who put it there, without a counterspell, and I can't see magic anymore to figure out if this one is different. That place in my head…isn't empty." Her emotions sloughed into wonder. "I'm not alone there."

That place…?

…*Is where I am,* his own dragon crooned. *This is what I guard.*

Kenth had never considered it a place, or thought about it much at all, his dragon was so much a part of himself. A part that Mackenzie had been missing for all these years.

"It's kind of amazing, isn't it?" he said.

"She's...we're...it's not always like words."

Kenth could feel her joy and he gave his own dragon a wave of amorphous appreciation.

After another lengthy kiss, Kenth sighed. "We should get back," he said regretfully. "No one knows what happened to us."

"I don't know how we'll get back up that," Mackenzie said, looking up the bluff that they'd come down. "And I won't be able to see or resist any magical traps."

"We can go on foot," Kenth said. "The cold won't bother us."

"The road meets the river eventually," Mackenzie said, gazing down the narrow canyon of snow-covered trees. "But it's going to be quite a hike to get to it." She looked at him suspiciously. "What did you just think of?"

Kenth realized he was going to be careful of his own train of thought now. "I thought maybe I could ride you," he said drolly. "And that led to another idea."

Mackenzie blinked at him without understanding, then realized, "I'm a dragon!" and she laughed out loud in delight. "Kenth, I'm a dragon! I can be a *dragon!*"

She backed away from Kenth several steps. "How do I do it, exactly?" she asked, and then Kenth was being shoved back into a snowbank by a wall of dragonhide as she filled considerably more space than she had anticipated. With a chirp of chagrin, she stepped gracefully away. She offered a front claw to help him as he struggled back up out of the snow and then was human again, standing some distance away, wide-eyed with delight and alarm. "Sorry!" she said. "I'm a dragon!"

"Rub it in, why don't you," Kenth said, without a shred of actual jealousy. Watching her revel in her new existence was as rewarding as if he'd been the one who was suddenly a magical creature. How amazing would it be to spend your entire life thinking you were broken and alone and then *be a dragon?*

"Can I fly with you?" Mackenzie asked, glancing up again. A bird or a gust of wind knocked a clump of snow down on her face and she sputtered and wiped it aside.

"Probably better not," Kenth said practically. "There's kind of a knack to it, and I'd like to not be accidentally dropped because you forgot how claws worked while you were figuring out how wings work."

"I'd feel really bad if I dropped you," Mackenzie agreed.

"I'd know how bad you felt," Kenth teased her.

"I'd know that you knew how bad I felt," she said merrily. "Well, let's figure out how you can ride me, and maybe we'll get back in time to tuck Dalaya in."

Kenth looked up the bluff again. "How…how did you do that? How did you catch me?"

Mackenzie followed his gaze. "I don't know for sure, but I think that Amara cast a spell on me when I was very young, hoping to shortcut me, as she did with Dalaya. To protect me, my mother bound my dragon and all magic away from me, and Amara's spell lay dormant behind its walls until the protection of it was gone."

"Should I be worried for Dalaya?"

Mackenzie's face betrayed her wonder even before Kenth felt it through their bond. "My dragon says no," she said in awe. "But she won't say why. Is your dragon always this…?" She flapped her hands helplessly.

"Obtuse? Annoying? Smug?" Kenth knew the feeling well. "Get used to that!"

CHAPTER 32

The trip back to civilization was not without its hazards.

Four limbs were a lot to keep track of and twice Mackenzie spread her wings out instinctively to keep her balance and then had to figure out how to fold them back before she knocked over too many trees or hurt herself.

She stepped through frozen ice into the river at one point and nearly pitched Kenth off into the overflow, then shifted suddenly back to human and Kenth fell the height of a dragon directly on top of her, knocking her flat and cracking the ice all around them. For a bad moment, Mackenzie nearly panicked, sure that they were both going to drown, then she was standing ankle-deep in the rushing water as a dragon realizing that it couldn't endanger her.

Kenth, rather water-logged, scrambled back up on her back and she hoped that her chagrin and apology was clear through their link, since she couldn't speak to him as a dragon.

"It's okay," he hastened to say. "I probably did worse

when I was learning to walk. Of course, I wasn't two stories tall or carrying anyone when I was still learning."

She shifted back to human when they got to the road; although Mackenzie guessed that her natural cloaking would kick in and keep people from seeing her clearly, she wasn't sure what they would make of Kenth on her back—would her cloaking cover him?—and there was very little shoulder. The last thing she wanted to do was cause a dragon-car accident. Two feet were also a lot easier for her to manage, and she was getting tired.

She and Kenth staggered wearily through the slushy snow, hand in hand.

It wasn't long before a truck stopped. "Oh my gosh, are you guys okay?" the driver, a gray-haired woman, asked. "Are you *wet?* Good heavens, get in, there's a blanket in the back."

Mackenzie remembered to pretend to shiver as Kenth deftly explained that they were tourists from Alaska so they were used to the cold, but gosh, would they appreciate a ride to the next town and the use of a phone, topped with a winning smile that would have melted harder hearts than hers.

Mackenzie was in the back and the heater, blowing full blast, was noisy, so she couldn't hear much of Kenth's conversation on the phone. The driver cast him looks that got more suspicious and wondering with every exchange.

"Thank you so much," Kenth said sincerely, putting the phone back in the console. "I'm afraid that was an international call, you will of course be reimbursed handsomely as soon as I'm back home."

Mackenzie thought that the driver was going to take them straight off the road staring at Kenth. "You're one of those Alaskan princes!"

"Indeed, ma'am," Kenth said respectfully. "We appreciate your help very much."

Mackenzie caught the woman's eyes in the rearview mirror. "Are you a princess?"

"No, I'm a dragon," Mackenzie said quietly because she was punch drunk and it was still so new and wonderful.

"I'm sorry, what?" the driver said in complete innocence.

"No!" Mackenzie repeated, grinning. "I'm not a princess."

"She will be," Kenth assured the woman, "just as soon as I convince her to marry me."

The woman driving made a noise like a kettle whistling, and Mackenzie was pretty sure that she was completely delighted. She could tell that Kenth was.

"Are you *asking* me to marry you?" Mackenzie asked, and she had to repeat herself over the rattling heater fan.

Kenth twisted in his seat and looked back at her. "Yes," he said. "Will you marry me and come back with me to Alaska forever?"

Mackenzie let her joy and happiness flood through their bond as her only answer.

The driver, knuckles white on the wheel, demanded shrilly, "Aren't you going to answer him? Honey, I am *dying* here. This is better than the soaps."

"Yes," Mackenzie said wholeheartedly. Then, louder, "Yes, I'll marry you."

Kenth unbuckled himself and leaned back through the seats to kiss her. Mackenzie had to unbuckle her own seatbelt to meet him. The woman who had picked them up lay on the horn and hollered in happiness, then scolded them about getting their seatbelts back on before they all crashed and died in a fiery wreck.

Mackenzie fell asleep in the back seat as they drove to

town, lulled by the noise and the motion, and the feeling of Kenth in her head, her dragon purring inside her like an oversized cat in a stream of sunlight.

∽

"I've decided that I'm not that fond of flying in planes," Mackenzie confessed. "Even if I do like the cookies."

They landed in Fairbanks in the dark, orange just staining the horizon over the mountains. Was it sunrise or sunset? Mackenzie could not figure out what time it actually was.

An honor guard and limousine met them on the tarmac, along with Tray, Leinani, and Fask.

"Where's Dalaya?" Kenth demanded at once.

The others exchanged uncertain glances and Mackenzie felt Kenth's heart seize in panic right along with hers. Had Amara already come back to try again for her prize? Did she have *another* portal anchor in the palace? Where were they coming from?

Kenth advanced on Fask. "Where's my daughter?!"

Fask held his ground but swiftly raised both hands. "She's fine!" he said, sounding irritated. "We left her at the castle."

"There's been…a complication," Leinani said carefully, gazing pointedly at the stewardess who was standing in earshot.

"What *kind* of complication?" Kenth demanded in a low growl. "Is she hurt? What's wrong?"

Through their new two-way bond, Mackenzie could feel his concern for Dalaya and all of his mistrust and resentment of his brother…but it was less than she had expected it to be, mellowed by time and other affections.

Some of his anger was more habit than active dislike, and he had underlying devotion that made it all more tangled.

She took Kenth's hand and earned a wave of his gratitude, even though he didn't let his stare at Fask waver.

"Let's talk privately," Fask said, turning to stalk back to the limo.

Leinani was carrying a coat, and she offered it to Mackenzie, who smiled and shrugged. "I don't need it," she said, feeling a swell of wonder and joy as her dragon chuckled in her head. She wondered belatedly if she should have taken it to maintain their charade.

I have always kept you warm, her dragon said lovingly. *Even when I could not be there with you.*

Leinani gave her a politely puzzled look and Mackenzie could not keep herself from leaning forward and saying, as quietly as she could muster, "I have a *dragon.*"

Fask was out of earshot already but Tray stared in wonder. "A dra—!" Leinani pinched him a reminder and he snapped his mouth closed.

Then he gave a shout of laughter that seemed over the top even for that news and offered Mackenzie a fist. It took her a moment to remember what a fistbump was and she tapped it shyly with her own.

They made their way to the limo and the door was barely shut behind them before Kenth was demanding of Fask, "What happened to Dalaya?"

"It's an embarrassment of dragons," Tray said merrily, clearly very amused by something. "A whole bevy of them!"

Fask gave him a quelling look. "I don't know why you'd say *that,*" he said crossly.

"Dalaya is a dragon now," Leinani said evenly.

Mackenzie could genuinely not tell what was her own astonishment and what was Kenth's.

"She shifted?" he asked eagerly. "I missed her first shift?"

"About fifty pounds of dragonhide and claws," Tray said. "I'm sorry you weren't there! It was the most adorable thing I've ever seen. One minute, she's wrestling with Moose over a bone, the next she's got four legs. The puppies took great offense over the fact that she has wings and they don't."

"We didn't dare bring her with us," Leinani said with a kind smile. "Not until she's got some more control over her shifting."

"I sympathize," Mackenzie said, remembering how she'd inadvertently shifted with Kenth on her back. They exchanged rueful smiles. "Maybe we can learn to fly together."

"What are you talking about?" Fask looked puzzled and rather put out.

Kenth put his hand protectively over Mackenzie's. "She's a dragon. She was a dragon all along, it had just been locked away from her by her mother, to protect her. She's a dragon, and she's going to be my wife." There was challenge in his voice, strumming down the mate bond between them.

He was expecting Fask to disbelieve it, Mackenzie thought, or deny it in some way.

But Fask only said in shock, "Congratulations."

Tray's congratulation was rather more sincere, and Leinani's was warm and genuine.

"Do you know who your parents were?" Leinani asked. "There aren't that many dragon families."

Mackenzie shook her head reluctantly. "I still have a lot of questions," she confessed. Kenth's hand tightened on her. "But I have some memories to start from, now. Not many, and they're *fuzzy*, but it's more than I ever had before."

I kept them safe for you, her dragon said, and for a moment, Mackenzie was completely full of love—Kenth's love, her dragon's love, her mother's love…even her own love. She could look at herself and not think that she was an aberration or a monster.

She was Mackenzie.

And she was a *dragon*.

CHAPTER 33

The next day, the caster of the guard removed the hateful necklace. The moment he was free, Kenth took Mackenzie and Dalaya to fly in short bursts in the broad field behind the castle at first, one at a time, where snowbanks could cushion crash landings.

Kenth explained the technique, how each wing was independent, how every little adjustment had a big effect. "It's really easy to overcorrect," he warned them. "Think about making tiny, tiny changes."

Dalaya bounced in place on two legs, eager to go up. "I'm a dragon! Tiny changes!"

He demonstrated again, shifting, then jumping up as he spread his wings. Dalaya squealed in the backdraft and cried, "Me, me, me!"

"Wait!" Mackenzie reminded her. "We're taking turns!"

She was no less excited, Kenth knew, as he landed at the far end of the snowfield and waited.

He couldn't hear them from this distance, even with dragon hearing, but he could feel the hum of Mackenzie's anticipation and see Dalaya shift into a dark shape twice the mass of her human form and spread sail-like wings. Mackenzie helped her position them for take-off and crouch.

Dalaya was having trouble with the leap needed for liftoff, but she gamely tried, again and again, until she had enough loft to fly to Kenth, crash-landing at his feet to bounce up as a human girl. "Again!" she cried. "Again!"

Mackenzie's short flight was flawless. Kenth wasn't sure if it was because she had more experience with her usual limbs than Dalaya did, or if she simply had more self-control. She landed delicately, winging down on her back legs and then dropping to her front. Everything about her felt like joy and triumph.

"More!" Dalaya crowed. Before they could stop her, she was shifting and flinging herself up into the air to glide a short distance and face-plant into a snowbank. Kenth chased her down and tickled her into human form so she could scream with laughter, while Mackenzie took to the air above them and practiced banking and diving.

Dalaya turned back into a dragon and hopped impatiently.

Kenth gave Dalaya a boost into the air and she beat her wings and climbed higher than she'd gotten before, gliding and skimming at the surface of the snow. She misjudged the time to start flapping again, or perhaps her own distance from the ground, and plowed into a dune of snow, emerging as a girl again, laughing and saying, "Trow me again! Wheee!"

They practiced until Dalaya was clumsy with exhaustion, then took her inside for a well-earned rest. She protested that she didn't need or want a nap, but lay down obediently and was sound asleep before Mackenzie and Kenth could even leave.

CHAPTER 33

It was fascinating how she could be so full of life and energy one moment and sleeping like a rag doll the next. "Do we have to worry about her magic?" Kenth asked quietly. "Or yours?"

Mackenzie looked distant, perhaps consulting with her dragon. "Amara's spell was meant for someone with dragon's blood, and I think that she assumed it was like the focus stone and would only work on children. It was one of the spells she never let me see or I might have told her otherwise. It was dormant in me until my dragon was freed, and in Dalaya...she *will* still be able to do magic, but her dragon should be able to keep her from using it *accidentally*. We can learn our limitations together. It isn't the bottomless and lawless power that Amara imagined and wanted to control, but I don't know exactly how it works yet. It was several days between Dalaya's spells and I couldn't do anything with it yesterday after I'd saved you. It feels like there's a recharge cycle."

"Amara could still try to come for her," Kenth said, gazing down at his sleeping daughter. "And maybe for the other kids. There's still someone here, in the castle, who set those portal anchors, and we don't know if they have more of them."

"We'll stop her first," Mackenzie said fiercely. "We will find her, and we will keep her from using anyone else, ever. The Compact will be renewed, and we will keep everyone safe."

Kenth loved this sexy, confident new Mackenzie who was sure of herself and her place so much that he had to kiss her. She gladly stepped to kiss him back, but when he might have pulled her into the bedroom, he felt her hesitation. "Do you want to go fly some more?" he guessed.

"Do you mind?" Mackenzie said hopefully. "I mean, it's probably old hat to you, but..."

She didn't have to explain. Kenth knew how it felt to claim the sky. "Let's go." He texted to have Mrs. James check in on Dalaya and took Mackenzie by the hand.

They scurried down the hall and out, laughing and leaping from the porch to spread wings and soar up into the clear winter sky. It was early afternoon, the sun already dipping to kiss the horizon with all the colors of the world, but it sank at such a slow angle that the sky would stay bright for hours.

They couldn't speak, flying in dragon form, but they could play chase and follow games, Mackenzie testing her limits. Kenth had all of her joy and rapture and mirth in his mind, and they tumbled and banked and raced and climbed higher into the sky.

Her awe was almost tangible in his head when they fell into a high, easy glide. Below them, wild Alaska stretched out in every direction. Even Fairbanks looked tiny and lost in the landscape of snow and mountains.

Impulsively, Kenth peeled away from their lazy circles and let Mackenzie follow him towards the northern mountains. He led her into a high mountain pass, then further, to a spectacular cliff with a flat, wind-scoured top. He landed there, wondering if he'd given her too great a challenge; the winds were tricky in the mountains, but the view was worth it.

Mackenzie circled twice before she landed, testing the wind gusts and her own control before she settled—just a little heavily—to land beside Kenth.

They shifted to human form almost simultaneously, and she laughed in glee as she closed the space between them and threw her arms around him. "You gave me the sky," she said, tearfully grateful and glad.

"It was always yours," Kenth told her. "And no one can take it from you now."

A gust of wind lifted her braid from the back of her coat. She looked down over the edge. "Is this where you and your brothers come to cliff-jump?"

Kenth nodded. "This was where Tray and Leinani were captured." It occurred to him to ask, "That spell isn't active anymore, is it?"

"I can't tell for sure anymore," Mackenzie said, staring down thoughtfully. "But I remember thinking it would only work the once. It was a pretty big spell, and it was set when Amara didn't have a dragon at her disposal."

"Could you stop it?" Kenth wanted to know. "With your own magic, I mean?"

Mackenzie closed her eyes. "I think I could," she said, with dawning confidence. "And I think that if something caught us, it would be very, very sorry that it did."

"Want to see if you can catch me this time?" Kenth asked with a cheeky grin, and he dived off the cliff to turn into a dragon, shooting straight down for the snowy canyon below them.

"This is not a plan!" she hollered after him gleefully, and then she was following, her beautiful dragon form like an arrow after him. This time, she flew flawlessly, strong and sure of herself.

They played touch and fly games through the canyon and back up into the sky until he languidly led Mackenzie back in starlight to the castle where his brothers waited with dinner.

Kenth hadn't realized what it would mean to have family again, or how much he had missed it.

Now he was coming home with his mate, to his daughter, and the sky was theirs, forever.

A NOTE FROM ELVA BIRCH

Thank you for reading The Dragon Prince's Secret. This series has been such a wild ride and I hope you are enjoying it as much as I'm enjoying writing it. I can't wait to dig in to Raval's adventures. (He's going to be so crabby with me...)

Your reviews are very much appreciated; I read them all and they help other readers decide whether or not to buy my books! A huge thank you to all of my fabulous beta readers and copy editors; any errors that remain are entirely my own. If you find typos — or you'd just like share your thoughts with me! — please feel free to email me at elvaherself@elvabirch.com.

Find out more about my books ad projects at: elvabirch.com

I also write under other pen names—keep reading for information about my other available titles...

MORE BY ELVA BIRCH

A Day Care for Shifters: A hot new full-length series about adorable shifter kids and their struggling single parents in a town full of mystery and surprise. Start the series with Wolf's Instinct, when Addison comes to Nickel City to take a job at a very special day care and finds a family to belong to. A gentle ice-cream-straight-from-the-container escape. Sweet and sizzling!

~

The Royal Dragons of Alaska: A fascinating alternate world where Alaska is ruled by secret dragon shifters. Adventure, romance, and humor! Reluctant royalty, relentless enemies…dogs, camping, and magic! Start with The Dragon Prince of Alaska.

~

Suddenly Shifters: A hilarious series of novellas, serials, and shorts set in the small town of Anders Canyon, where something (in the water?) is making ordinary citizens turn into shifters. Start with Something in the Water! Also available in audio!

∾

Birch Hearts: An enchanting collection of short stories and novellas. Unconstrained by theme or setting, each short read has romance, magic, and heart, with a satisfying conclusion. And always, the impossible and irresistible. Start with a sampler plate in Prompted 2 for fourteen pieces of sweet-to-sizzling flash fiction, or dive in with the novella, Better Half. Breakup is a free story!

WRITING AS ZOE CHANT

Shifting Sands Resort: A complete ten-book series - plus two collections of shorts. This is a thrilling shifter romance set at a tropical island resort. Each book stands alone but connects into a great mystery with a thrilling conclusion. Start with Tropical Tiger Spy or dive in to the Omnibus edition, with all of the novels, short stories, and novellas in my preferred reading order!

∾

Fae Shifter Knights: A complete four-book fantasy portal romp, with cute pets and swoon-worthy knights stuck in a world of wonders like refrigerators and ham sandwiches. Start with Dragon of Glass!

∾

Green Valley Shifters: A sweet, small town series with single dads, secret shifters, sweet kids, and spinsters. Lowperil and steamy! Standalone books where you can revisit your favorite characters - this series is also complete! Start with Dancing Barefoot! Green Valley Shifters crosses over with **Virtue Shifters**. Start with Timber Wolf!

A SNEAK PREVIEW OF THE DRAGON PRINCE'S MAGIC

༄༅

Raval came warily from the garage, glancing in both directions and pausing to listen for laughter.

The castle was *infested* with children.

It wasn't just Kenth's little curly-haired demon daughter, with her shrill demands and enchanted pictures; there were about a dozen of the monsters living in the family halls while the search continued for their proper families or suitable foster care.

It was an absolute minefield to get from Raval's workshop in the garage to his rooms in the main house.

Sometimes, they were playing out in the snow, happy to pelt anyone walking by with showers of snow, screeching and chasing and making a hazard out of every walkway. They were worse than Tray's dogs when they were loose.

When it was too cold for human children to be outside, they were running down the halls and sliding in their socks —several times with Toren, who seemed to accept that with *three* other brothers tapped with mates, he could not possibly need to be considered the king-in-waiting any longer and had reverted to his own childhood. His mate, Carina, did nothing to rein him in and had been caught more than once sliding down the banisters.

The little people stormed up and down the stairs like herds of very tiny and irritating moose, constantly underfoot and braying.

Raval made it to the house unmolested and when he heard a stampede of small feet in the west wing, took the long way around to the front hall in order to avoid them.

He was unsuccessful.

One of the young people was sitting on the stairs up to his rooms. It was the oldest one, Raval thought, a boy on reluctant cusp of adulthood.

He might have made it safely past and up to his rooms, but the boy gave a noisy sigh of misery and Raval closed his eyes and dredged inside his chest for patience. This was a situation that called for empathy. These kids were refugees from a madwoman's magic cult. They'd been forced to make spells—sloppy, dangerous spells—like they were in some kind of enchantment factory run on child labor and artifacts.

He just wished they were someone else's problem right now.

"Are you okay?" he asked gruffly.

The boy stared at him without response.

"I heard they were going to get you a teacher," Raval said, desperately grasping at conversational straws.

This, however, appeared to be the exact wrong thing to say.

"She won't like me," the boy said miserably. Randal was his name, Raval remembered suddenly. "And Mackenzie says I might have to go away, anyway."

"Why wouldn't the teacher like you?" Raval asked, trying to sound jovial. It took him a moment to recognize that the boy was still staring at him without looking away. That was the kind of thing that bothered most other people, and Raval had grudgingly learned not to do it himself in order to fit in, but he'd bet half his hoard that Randal wasn't entirely neurotypical.

Like Raval himself.

The sympathy he'd had to look for was all he felt now. It was a *lot* to face the world knowing that you were out of step with everyone else. But Raval was very sure, "They aren't going to hire a teacher that won't like you. Believe me, Fask will pick the very best of the best. She'll be a Mary Poppins, wait and see."

"What's a Mary Poppins?" Randal asked.

Raval thought he said it sullenly, but Raval rarely read emotion correctly into other people, so it probably wasn't. These kids hadn't been exposed to much modern media, so he assumed the question was genuine.

"Mary Poppins is practically perfect in every way," Raval quoted. "She's a magical nanny who comes to teach children to use their imagination. She was in a book before the movie."

"I'm magical," Randal said thoughtfully. "Is that Mary Poppins?"

A woman with bouncy black curls had just come around the corner at the bottom of the stairs and something inside of Raval seemed to snap into place.

Raval was used to being a few steps behind everyone else. He remembered people's names late in every conversation and laughed at jokes after they weren't funny anymore. He realized only now that his feeling of urgency when he left his garage sanctuary had not been to the purpose of evading children, but to being here, in this place, to meet this woman at this moment.

He looked at her critically, trying to decide what it was

about her that appealed to him so completely. There was something about her mouth, about how red and full her lips were, something about her curly, dark hair. There was something about her figure—is that what books referred to as lush? There was something about her dancing brown eyes. There was something about all of her that was absolutely, undeniably...practically perfect.

"Well, hello," she said cheerfully. She looked a little confused, like she'd been expecting someone else and been pleasantly surprised. She *felt* a little confused, Raval realized. He could *feel* her reaction to him.

She was confused, and she was *dazzled*.

Raval actually had to look around, to make sure she wasn't looking at one of his brothers standing behind him.

"You're Raval, aren't you?" she said, sounding breathless. *Feeling* breathless. She bounded up the few steps separating them and extended her hand. "I'm Tara. I'm here... well, I thought I was here to act as a live-in nanny and teacher for a while, but I think I'm here to meet *you*. I'm sorry, that's the wildest thing, isn't it?"

"No," Raval said hesitantly. "It's not."

He realized belatedly that he was supposed to shake her hand and he shyly slipped his hand into hers.

The touch of her skin on his was like electricity. But good electricity, warm and welcome. He could hold onto that hand for the rest of time. This was what he'd been put on this earth to do, to hold that hand and fall down into those eyes.

Fortunately, Tara actually knew how a handshake was supposed to go, and she gave his arm a cheerful couple of pumps and extracted herself before Raval could make it weird.

"I'm sorry," he said.

"For what?" Tara laughed. "Never apologize if you don't mean it."

She was so joyful, Raval thought. He'd never thought much about happiness, but this woman was his, he thought. His whole world was brighter and broader and safer. He was filled with relief and his dragon was whispering in his ear urgently.

He had to concentrate to make words out of the swirl of feelings inside him.

...our one! Our destiny!

"Are you Tara Poppins?" Randal asked. Raval had nearly forgotten he was there.

Tara's laughter was like music, Raval thought. Really good music. "I can be," she said kindly. "You must be Randal. I'm looking forward to teaching you and I hope we'll get along well."

But she turned back to Raval even as she spoke, drawn like a magnet. The same magnet that was drawing Raval to her.

Raval didn't always trust his own conclusions. He knew that he saw the world a little differently than most people, and what seemed obvious to others was obtuse to him, just like things that he thought were completely undeniable seemed outside of the grasp of others' understanding.

This was not a conclusion he could deny.

"You're my mate," he blurted.

"Okay," Tara said cheerfully. "What's that?"

Continue the tale in *The Dragon Prince's Magic*!